EMMA'S FOLLY

EMMA'S FOLLY

•

Carolyn Brown

AVALON BOOKS
NEW YORK

PRINTED IN THE UNITED STATES OF AMERICA
ON ACID-FREE PAPER
BY HADDON CRAFTSMEN, BLOOMSBURG, PENNSYLVANIA

Chapter One

Emma Maureen Cummins felt faint as she stepped off the train in Guthrie, Oklahoma. Precious little had to do with the fact that she hadn't eaten in almost twenty-four hours. Nor was it the stifling hot wind blowing in her face. Even less had anything to do with the tight-fitting jacket she wore. The reality of her impetuousness came full circle when she looked at the little red frame building serving as a train station, and the rest of the town still in the first throes of massive growth. For the first time in three days, she realized just what her fit of anger had reaped.

She pulled the sweeping skirt of her dark burgundy dress to one side and checked her reflection in the window of a dress shop. Maybe she should open the door and ask the owner if she was interested in hiring someone to sew for her. No, she shook her head. Not right now. She might do that later, but not today.

At least she still looked reasonably presentable, which

was a miracle after two days of sleeping in a sitting posi-
tion. In a town still bursting at the seams with so many
new people, no one would take notice of one more face,
and there had to be at least one job somewhere. At least
that's what she'd planned while her anger boiled and fes-
tered since she left Georgia. She took a deep breath and
crossed the tracks gingerly. She could see a few bigger
buildings. Perhaps one of them needed a woman with just
her skills.

Which are? her conscience chided.

"Oh, hush. I can cook, sew, give piano lessons, even
teach if I have to," she whispered aloud and drew herself
up to her full height of five feet eleven inches. A formidable
woman, with a halo of golden hair pulled up into a fash-
ionable bun on top of her head. She checked her reflection
in a store window. Not too bad. A few curls escaping from
her hair pins, but at least she didn't look like a hoyden.

The word brought back memories of the awful argument.
Well, she'd sure enough won the fight, hadn't she? She'd
told them both that she didn't need a husband; wouldn't
have a father who dictated what she'd do with her life; and
she could well take care of herself.

"Doing what?" Her father had sneered. "You're nothing
but a hoyden most days. Your mother spoiled you rotten
and since her death, you've gotten even more unladylike.
You're going to do what I say for once in your life, Emma
Maureen, or else. This is for your own good. You are
twenty years old. Folks are already saying you're a crazy
old maid."

"I am not getting married," she'd told him. "Not until I
find someone I truly love, and I don't love Matthew."

"Love has little to do with a marriage," her father had
said seriously. "You've got two days, Emma Maureen, to
tell Matthew you'll marry him within the next six months.
You'll have a husband before your twenty-first birthday."

"Or what?" she had asked.

"Or I'll leave this entire plantation to charity before I

leave it to a crazy old maid who has no idea how to run it. Matthew will take care of everything I've worked all my life for. He'll be the son I never had. The father of a whole bunch of grandsons, I hope."

"You wouldn't!" she'd whispered in fear. Jefferson William Cummins never made a threat. He simply stated facts.

"I will," he'd sworn seriously. "You will have a place to live as long as I live, but when I'm gone you'll be on your own. Two days, Emma Maureen. This conversation is over. It's your decision."

"Miss Emma, I'll make you a good husband." Matthew had smiled up from the chair where he sat. He was three inches shorter than Emma, had thinning blond hair attempting to cover a freckled scalp and beady little eyes the same sickening brown as the suit he wore.

Matthew Cross didn't fool Emma one bit. He was more interested in the thousands of acres that made up the cotton growing plantation of Crooked Oaks than he was Emma. When he looked at her, she felt like he was assessing her for a slave block. She couldn't imagine shedding her josie, much less her drawers, and crawling into bed with Matthew. Just the thought of him even kissing her turned her stomach. She not only didn't love him; she didn't like him.

Matthew drew deeply on his cigar and blew the smoke out slowly. "You'll only have to give up your bicycle and those novels you read. Those two things just aren't fitting for a married woman. Of course, after the first year you'll have a child each year to take care of and I'm sure you'll see the wisdom in the mother of my children not behaving like your father said, in a hoyden manner. I won't pressure you for an answer right now. I have every confidence when you have time to think about it, you'll come to your senses and realize it's your only option. I'll give you a couple of days to make your decision."

Her decision had been to take what money she had of her very own and spend it on a ticket to Enid, Oklahoma. She'd been intrigued by the land run the year before and had read everything she could find about it. If her father cared enough to search for her, the ticket agent would tell him she'd purchased a ticket to Enid. She had no intentions of going there. She was stopping in Guthrie and Jefferson Cummins would never find her in Enid when he sent someone to search for her.

If he did. By now Crooked Oaks was most likely already destined for charity.

Surely, the people in Guthrie would be liberal in their views. She'd simply find a job, live in a boarding house and show her father just exactly how independent she could be. The first item on the list was to find a job. She smoothed the front of her jacket, fluffed out the peplum ruffle around her slim waist, and took a deep breath as she opened the door of the general store. Everyone had to have flour, sugar, and coffee, so it stood to reason if there were jobs in town the proprietor would know about them. Perhaps he even needed a nice tall crazy old maid to stock his shelves or sell yard goods to the female population of Guthrie and the surrounding areas. If not, she'd try asking door to door, starting with the dressmaking shop.

Just inside the door, a tall man with a badge on his chest and a shock of silver hair stared at her from beneath heavy gray eyebrows. The badge declared him to be the sheriff. The eyes bored at her with so much intensity, Emma felt like he could see all the way to the bottom of her soul. A cold chill shot up her spine in spite of the warm spring day. She shook off the feeling of doom and brushed past the sheriff and his insolent looks.

"Jed, you needin' chicken feed, too?" A man said at the back of the store.

"Give me two sacks. I think that might do it for this month. Maybe even for a couple of months. Got one more stop to make and then it's back to the old homestead," the younger man said.

"Excuse me, ma'am, did you just get off the train by any

chance?" The sheriff asked in a booming voice, his mouth moving very little beneath a heavy gray mustache.

The young man turned around to see who the sheriff was talking to. The woman was so close to him he could see every faint freckle across her cute, turned up nose. She was the only female he'd ever known, other than his sister, who could look him right in the eye. Which she did, and didn't blink even once.

Nothing had scared Emma since the day she was five years old and figured out spiders could be stepped on and smashed flat. From that time she faced life the same way. If it got in her way, she found a way over or around it. If she couldn't do that, then she simply smashed it. Just like Matthew. She couldn't get around him. She wouldn't marry him, so she left. It was her way of smashing the whole marriage idea. But this sheriff just plain put a cold knot of fear in her with his searching eyes and one question which she had no intention of answering.

"Jed, darling." She ignored the sheriff as if he was nothing more than the barrel of dry beans he stood beside . . . or a spider. The young man was staring at her with a question in his eyes she hoped the sheriff couldn't see. Without taking her pale aqua eyes from his mossy green ones, she smiled. "I got tired of waiting in the buggy. Are we about ready to go?"

"You know this lady, Jed?" The sheriff raised an eyebrow.

Please help me. She mouthed the words silently. She was sandwiched between the two men. The blue-eyed sheriff behind her, looking over her shoulder at Jed; the handsome, green-eyed cowboy in front of her. She'd felt like she'd just been tossed into a raging river. It was definitely time to drown or swim, and Emma Cummins wasn't going to drown this late in the game.

"Of course," Jed said.

"You sure? I got a telegram to be on the lookout for a tall blond from Atlanta, Georgia. She's a runaway. Telegram from her father says she's not right. Kinda flighty and slow witted. If I find her I'm to lock her up until he can get here and claim her. Machinery went down at the end of the telegram so we didn't get her name. Did say the daughter had purchased a ticket to Enid, Oklahoma but he was sending notices to most places between here and Atlanta. Lines are likely down between here and Tulsa again is the reason we didn't get the rest of the message. Probably have it fixed in a couple of hours." The sheriff looked over her shoulder at Jed, who was grinning like a lovesick puppy.

Please, she mouthed again.

" 'Course I know her. Picked her up at the train station while ago and we're on our way to the church to get the preacher man to marry us. You know how I been strugglin' to get along these past months out there on the place. You ever heard of a mail-order bride, Sheriff?" Jed said and Emma's heart sank down into her button-top shoes.

"Well, if that ain't the durnest thing," the sheriff said. "Got every young filly in Logan County talkin' about you and you done got one of them brides from the mailman. If it don't beat all. Well, boy, I don't believe you." The smile was gone in an instant from the sheriff's face and replaced by a frown.

"Sorry, Sheriff. It's the truth," Jed said.

"I think you just now this minute laid eyes on that woman. What's her name?"

Emma, she mouthed.

"First name is Emma. Last name don't matter, Sheriff, because in ten minutes she'll be Emma Thomas." Jed reached down and took her hand in his.

The touch glued him to the floor and caused all kinds of bells to go off in Emma's head. Surely it was caused by the lack of food. She just hadn't felt like eating that last day on the train. Besides, there was no such thing as love at first sight or first touch either. Things like that only happened in Kate Chopin's novels of romance down on the Louisiana bayous.

"Well, Jed, I'm going to call your bluff which I think it is. I'm the sheriff, but I'm also a justice of the peace. So just to be sure you ain't lyin' to me, son, I believe I'll just marry you two myself. Let's go over the jail house where I got some of the marriage forms. Josh, you and the missus got time to witness for us today?"

"Well, I think Emma had her heart set on a church wedding, if that's all right with you, but we'd be glad to have you come along and listen to the vows," Jed said as he turned Emma around to face the sheriff. "We're going to drive over in the wagon. Want to ride in the back with the chicken feed?"

Mercy, but what was he about to get himself into? Jed wondered. He sure didn't intend to marry anyone. Especially not a giant blond-haired woman who was on the run from something or someone. She didn't look like she was missing a few marbles, but then one couldn't tell by mere looks. Look at Maggie Liston. All that beautiful red hair and she could dance rings around every other girl at the barn dances. But that's as far as it went. To say that she was simple would be a gross understatement.

"No." The sheriff shook his head.

Jed's heart slowed down. He'd won. He'd called the sheriff's bluff. Now he and Emma-whoever-she-was could crawl into the wagon seat and he'd drive toward the church at the edge of town. Before they got there, he'd help her down like a gentleman and go on his merry way. She could get back on the train and go on hers.

"No," the sheriff repeated. "If you're getting married today, Jed, then I'm marrying you. That's the only choice you got. If you want me to wait a couple of hours for the next telegram to prove me wrong, then we'll just sit in the jail and wait. Then if you're on the up-and-up you can go to one of the churches and get hitched. If you're bluffing, this is the time to get out of it. I'll let you go on back to the homestead and hold this woman for her father. If you ain't, you'll be married in fifteen minutes and I'll file the papers at the courthouse just to keep it all legal. Tell me Emma, what part of the south are you from anyway?"

"Why, I'm from Savannah, sir," she said. The words came out in a soft, southern drawl that amazed her. She figured she'd not be able to utter a single word, that her voice would be nothing more than a high squeak. She wasn't going to marry this stranger, even if his fingertips did burn her hand and she could still hear bells ringing in her head. She'd tell the truth and be locked up in jail before she married someone she didn't even know. At least she knew exactly what Matthew expected of her. If she had to promise God that she would love, honor and obey any man, which she was not about to do, it would be with someone she knew.

It was a crying shame men had so much control in the world anyway. They could vote. They could own property and tell their daughters how to live their lives. It just plain wasn't fair.

"Savannah, huh? Well, let's get on over to the jail and take care of these vows. Jed, I'll be right behind you on my horse so don't try nothing foolish. One more time, are you bluffing? When we get to the jail your chances are over. I'll run you in for aiding and abetting a runaway, you know," the sheriff told him.

The wagon was parked in front of the store. Jed slipped his hands around Emma's slim waist and helped her up into the seat, then nodded toward the sheriff who was already mounted and in place behind the wagon. He crawled up into his seat, slipped the reins between his fingers and slapped them gently against the horses' flanks. The wagon seat wasn't built to accommodate two people without them touching, so Jed's shoulder and Emma's were crammed together whether they liked it or not. She could sit close to him or fall out in the dirt. The red dust boiling up around the wheels of the wagon looked more and more inviting.

"We better stop this and tell the truth," Emma whispered without even glancing behind her. "I'm not about to marry you. I don't even know you except your name is Jed."

"And I don't know you either, except you said your name is Emma. But honey, you will marry me. I'm not going to jail for aiding and abetting anyone. The sheriff is just testing my mettle. He'll probably say it's all right for us to go on to get married in the church when we get to the jail, but if he starts saying the vows, you better stand right up there and say them. I don't want to marry you either, but it's the only thing that came to my mind, and we will get married before I'll be sitting in jail for aiding and abetting. Because I've got to be home before dark. I've got four kids waiting on me at home."

"Four kids?" Her eyes widened until they ached.

"Yep, four kids, and come to think of it they could sure use a grown-up female around the homestead," he said, grinning nervously. If the sheriff called his bluff, Anna Marie was going to go up in six-foot flames.

"This is not the time to joke around. Stop this wagon and let me out right now. I'll tell the sheriff it was all my idea," she said.

"And I lose my kids, my homestead and everything I've worked the last year for? He gave me more than one chance to stand up and tell the truth, and I lied. So my chances are gone and if he gets out his book and says, 'Do you?' then I'm saying 'I do!' Anyway, they'll just be pie-crust promises."

"What?" she asked.

"Pie-crust promises. Made to be broken. In a few weeks, you can simply get on the train to go visit your Savannah relatives and no one will be the wiser. I'll tell everyone this wasn't the life you thought it was. That you weren't cut out to be a farmer's wife and missed all your fancy southern friends and parties. You can get a divorce," he said.

"Oh, no," she whispered, moaning. Nice women didn't

get divorces. The boiling pot of water she'd gotten herself into just got hotter and hotter. Crooked Oaks just got left to a charity for doubly sure. Oh, well, at least Matthew wouldn't get his grimy little paws on the plantation. She'd just as soon see it all go to charity as see his beady little eyes surveying the cotton crop.

"Oh, yes," Jed said. Good grief, if he hadn't stopped in at the lumber yard to price the wood to add a room on to the house, he would have already been on his way back home. One little fifteen-minute visit with Eb Mason and he was on his way to the jail to get married. Fitting place for a wedding, he thought. Balls and chains were the same, whether they took away a man's natural freedom or his spiritual freedom. Lord, but he hated to face Anna Marie when he got home.

"Step right in here." The sheriff dismounted and led the way into the jail house. "Every now and then I get to practice my justice of the peace skills. Folks in a hurry or traveling through. Now where's my book?" He fished around in a desk drawer, pulling out a book and a long piece of paper with *Marriage License* written in fancy script lettering across the top. "And here's Josh and his missus to witness for us." He nodded toward the door.

Emma wondered if she fell on the floor in a dead faint, would they all rush for the doctor so she could run away? What was she going to do if this Jed Thomas expected her to be a real wife? Sleep with him? It was enough to make her feel faint, but for the life of her she couldn't will herself into a swoon.

"Stand right here." The sheriff motioned for the short, bald-headed man and his plump wife. "Dearly beloved, we are gathered here before God and these two witnesses to unite this couple in holy matrimony." He read from the leather-bound book in his hands. Surely, any moment Jed would stop the farce if he was really just bluffing.

"Do you Jed Thomas, take this woman, Emma?" He stopped to wait for her last name.

"Emma Cummins," she said.

"Yes, uh-huh, do you Jed Thomas take this woman, Emma Cummins, to be your lawfully wedded wife, to have and to hold, in times of sickness and joy . . ." he intoned in a monologue.

Jed really did want to stop the whole thing right then. He couldn't marry up with a perfect stranger, no matter how many men sent off for brides they'd never seen. "I do," he said without blinking and wondered where the words came from.

"Do you Emma Cummins, take Jed Thomas to be your lawfully wedded husband, to love, honor, and obey . . ." he read again.

Obey? The word pierced Emma's heart. To promise before God Himself to obey a man she didn't even know? Thank goodness they were pie-crust promises and could be broken, even if they did make her a marked woman forever. She half expected a mass of black clouds to cover the skies and lightning to start dancing around her in circles. She'd been brought up to firmly believe that one did not lie to God and here she was about to make vows to Him that she would stay married to Jed Thomas until death parted them. Lying vows. That had to be blowing the bottom out of that commandment stating Thou shalt not lie.

"I do," she said when the sheriff looked up at her.

"Then by the authority vested in me by Oklahoma laws, I pronounce you husband and wife. What God hath joined together, let no man put asunder. Jed, you may kiss your mail-order bride."

Jed intended to peck her briefly on the cheek, but in less time than it takes a gnat to blink, he changed his mind. He was entitled to one good kiss for the tongue-lashing Anna Marie was going to give him. Before she got finished he would have a blistered soul and probably the red imprint of her hand across his face to boot. One real kiss wasn't much payment but he'd have that much, at least.

He put his arms around her and drew her so close he

could feel her heart racing beneath her burgundy jacket. He looked deep into her eyes, seeing only anger laced with a faint touch of fear, and touched his lips to hers. The kiss rocked both of them to the bottom of their hearts. Jed had kissed lots of girls in his twenty-three years, but nothing prepared him for the emotions that soared through his body when he kissed his new bride. Emma figured kissing was grossly overrated except in Kate Chopin's romance stories. At least that's what Emma figured until that very moment. She came as close to fainting as she'd ever done in her life and had to hold onto the sheriff's desk for support when Jed released her.

"Well, now I guess I do believe you." The sheriff chuckled. "Josh, you and the missus sign right here and here and I'll just trot this to the court house on my way out of town. Got a prisoner to pick up down in the southern part of the state. Train will pull out of here in half an hour."

Emma bit her tongue to keep from sighing out loud. Thirty minutes. If only she'd gone into the dress shop. Or even the saloon for a sarsaparilla. The men might have gawked at her and the women might have gotten wind that she'd actually set foot inside a place like that and never have a thing to do with her. But she wouldn't be married right that moment. The sheriff would have been on his way out of town and by the time he got back she would be just another citizen.

"Thank you both." Jed shook hands with the general store owner and his wife. "We appreciate you taking time out of your busy day for this. Now we'll be getting along home and I'll see you all in a couple or three months. End of fall for sure. Got to lay in supplies for the winter."

"I hope you'll be very happy here." The short little lady smiled brightly at Emma. "It's going to be a great state someday. Folks are friendly for the most part and I hear Jed has a nice spread. When he comes to town for supplies you tag along with him. Maybe me and you could visit over a cup of tea in my back room."

"Thank you." Emma smiled but it didn't reach her blue eyes. Long before Jed came back to town for supplies she'd be gone. On a fast train headed west. Maybe to California. Never back to Georgia. Definitely not to Oklahoma again.

Chapter Two

Birds were singing and a bunch of little purple forget-me-nots bloomed in a pot just outside the general store. A perfect wedding day for a disastrous wedding. Not that Jed Thomas wasn't a handsome man with all that black hair and thick eyelashes framing mossy green eyes. It's just that Emma didn't intend to marry until she was in love. Breathtaking love, like Kate talked about in her books.

"You need to go back to the train station for your baggage?" Jed asked before he slapped the reins against the horses' flanks.

"I have a small trunk," she said, nodding.

Jed turned the horses around and with a cluck of his tongue headed them toward the train station. He'd just married the most unlikely woman he could have ever imagined. His idea of a perfect wife was one who barely came to his shoulder, who looked at him with so much love in her eyes that he could drown in it, and who was able to help him run his spread and raise those four rambunctious kids. One look at Emma told him she certainly didn't fit any of his criteria for a wife. She was only a couple of inches shorter than his six feet one inches. She looked at him like she could kick him all the way to Texas and enjoy doing it. Goodness only knew, anyone who dressed all fancy like that couldn't cook and do laundry. More than likely she'd be more trouble than all four kids combined.

"Well, I guess I was wrong," the sheriff said when he spotted Jed carrying the trunk from the train station out to his wagon. "I would've sworn the way that woman acted that you didn't know her from Eve. But if she's brought her things, I guess she's really not that runaway."

"I didn't know her from Eve," Jed said. "At least not until a few minutes before you offered to marry us."

"Why didn't you get that trunk when you got her?" The sheriff narrowed his eyes.

"Wanted it at the back of the wagon," Jed answered. "You know how womenfolk are. She'll want her things unloaded so she can get out what she needs for tonight. She'll have it in the house and empty before I get the chicken feed unloaded."

"Ain't it the truth," the sheriff said, grinning. "You know womenfolk pretty good for a bachelor man."

"I had a good teacher," Jed said. "Good day, Sheriff. Have a good trip."

"Won't be a good trip. Got a train robber the Pinkston men cornered down in the northern part of Texas. Going after him to bring him right back here to Guthrie. Hope the kids like Ella. That was her name, wasn't it?"

"Close enough," Jed said, toting the trunk out to the wagon. Just a little trunk, she'd said, but the thing weighed as much as a baby elephant.

Emma opened her parasol and held it over her head as Jed drove eastward out of Guthrie. Her mother would turn over in her grave if she saw the freckles on Emma's face. She might have been liberal in her views when it came to

raising a daughter, but she sure expected Emma to be a
lady. A lady didn't run away and travel with no escort. She
sure didn't marry a man she'd never met even if he did
kiss really good. *But Momma,* she argued silently, *a lady
shouldn't be forced to marry Matthew either.*

Now, wasn't that a crazy argument. She shook her head
slowly. She'd run away from being forced to marry a man
she didn't love and walked right into the same thing. Only
this time she was forced to marry a man she didn't even
know.

Jed had been raised to help a lady in distress, but his
father certainly never told him to go that far above the call
of duty. Talk about things getting plumb out of hand.
Surely he could have thought up another story. He could
have told the sheriff she was the new governess for the
children, or his cousin from the south who'd come to help
him through the crisis of raising four kids and running a
ranch. Anything but a mail-order bride. If he hadn't been
reading that silly story he found in a magazine in his sister's trunk, he probably wouldn't have even thought of that
idea. It had just popped out of his mouth and then he had
to stand behind it.

"Do you need to make any other stops?" Emma asked.
"You can let me off anywhere now. The sheriff should be
gone. Is there a boarding house in Guthrie? I could stay
there until I find a job. By the time the sheriff gets back I
could be on the train to Enid. I've still got the train ticket."

"Nope, I don't need to stop," he said. "And I expect
you'd better come on to the homestead with me. We'll
figure out a time frame for you to leave later. Want to tell
me what you're running from?"

"No," she said.

Jed had thought about another stop earlier in the day.
He'd seen a little locket in the window of Nettie's Dressmaking Business just around the corner from the general
store. Anna Marie would like it and she'd been nice enough
to watch after Molly all day long, and then come home

with the kids after school today. She'd probably have supper on the back of the stove when he got there. He shrugged
his shoulders. He was taking home a wife instead of a
locket. Anna Marie would rather have the locket, without
a single doubt.

Emma's stomach rumbled in protest. She hadn't bothered
to eat anything the night before and was so excited at the
prospect of reaching her destination that she couldn't force
herself to eat breakfast. Lunch was out of the question. She
might miss something important as the train rumbled on its
way to Guthrie. The town of promise where she was going
to show her father and Matthew both that she couldn't be
sold or bought.

"Hungry?" Jed asked.

"A little," she said.

"Miss dinner?"

She nodded. "I wasn't hungry last night and too excited
to eat breakfast or lunch."

"You mean you haven't eaten since yesterday at dinner
time?" He stopped the wagon and stared at her. Great Scot,
the woman was probably nigh onto a dead faint. She might
be big enough to do without a meal or two, but he sure
didn't want to have to pick her up if she fell off the wagon
seat and sprawled out in the dirt.

"No, I didn't eat dinner. I told you that. I had a chicken
salad sandwich for lunch. One of those soggy things on the
train," she said.

"Emma, lunch is dinner. Dinner is supper. You're in
Oklahoma. I've got some cheese and crackers left from my
lunch I brought along with me. And some beef jerky and
a biscuit left from breakfast. Here. Eat." He pulled a flour
sack from beneath the wagon seat and handed it to her.
"It's a spell until supper. When you get finished I've got
some coffee in a jar. It's cold but it's wet."

"Thank you," she said softly. The cheese was absolutely
wonderful. A rich, dark yellow with few holes. The cold
biscuit had been slathered with fresh cream butter early that

morning and smeared with wild plum jelly. It melted in her mouth and was even better than her cook's sugar cookies at Crooked Oaks.

"What kind of cheese is this?" she asked.

"Just cheese. We make it ourselves like we do everything else we can. Get more milk than we can use so we make cheese and cottage cheese and butter," he said.

"It's very good," she said.

"You're hungry," he answered.

"I could use a drink. Is there clean water somewhere?" She eyed the creek they were traveling beside. A red clay bank with a trickling stream running ten feet down. The water looked less inviting than the coffee.

"No, drink the coffee in the jar. It's good to have Bear Creek for the livestock to drink, but it's not fit for human consumption. We don't drink water from anything but our well," he said.

"You mean you don't have clean creek water?" She thought of the stream running through the plantation. She'd stopped her bicycle lots of times beside it and drank the cool water, using her hands as a dipper.

"It might be clean once in a while if there's a good rain and it's flowing good. But we don't take any chances, especially this time of year. Boil it, cook it, peel it, or don't eat it. Unless it's out of our well. It's clean water. Spring fed and not off the creek. Here's coffee," he said, pulling out a jar of coffee so black it looked thick enough to make mud pies.

She waited for him to find a cup, even a tin one, but he kept driving without even looking at her. Half the coffee was gone. That meant he'd drunk from the jar. She sighed and twisted the lid off. Her first day of liberation. She'd gotten married to man she didn't know. Felt her knees go to jelly when he kissed her. Now she had to drink out of the same jar he had. Liberation surely wasn't what she'd expected it to be.

The wagon trail was just two ruts in the fresh green

grass. Cottontail rabbits darted across the path and squirrels barked in the trees at the people disturbing their world. Strange, she didn't feel scared. In Kate's books, she should have been weeping and swooning. But then the heroines in Kate's books were seldom close to six feet tall and independent as Emma.

She'd never seen so many hills. Up and down, the wagon bumping in and out of holes, over bumps in the trail. If her liver wasn't shook loose by the time they got to this homestead he kept talking about, she'd be surprised. Oklahoma Territory was a far cry from what she'd imagined. She'd thought about green grass and rolling, beautiful countrysides. Not stunted scrub oak trees and red dust. She tilted her chin up in defiance and made herself a vow. Two days, she'd stay at this homestead place. Only two days and then she was leaving. If Jed Thomas wouldn't take her back to town, she'd walk and board the train to Enid, where she'd start all over again. Divorce wasn't even an option. She would never marry and then she wouldn't have to worry about it. If Jed Thomas wanted to marry another woman, he could get a divorce.

She stiffened her backbone and her resolve. Nothing could frighten Emma Cummins . . . Thomas. Not spiders or prospective husbands or even unwanted good-looking husbands. She was independent and she would tell him when she was leaving; not the other way around. Give that sheriff plenty of time to get out of town and she'd be right back in Guthrie. But only for a few moments before she boarded a train and left again.

"Whoa," Jed said.

The wagon came to an abrupt halt and Emma looked out from the edge of her parasol right into the eyes of a whole band of Indians on horseback. Their eyes were as black as their long hair and she shuddered.

"Afternoon John Whitebear," Jed said.

"Jed Thomas?" The Indian said, grinning from one ear to the other. "What you got here?"

"Meet my new wife, Emma Thomas." Jed introduced her. "Emma, this is my good friend, John Whitebear."

"Pleased to meet you," she said, only a little bit breathless.

"Thought you weren't having a squaw in your cabin?" John's dark eyes danced in merriment. "Seems like the last time we shared a bit of tobacco on your place you said you weren't interested in women."

"Man can change his mind," Jed said.

"Very quickly," John said. "Maybe we will stop back by your place. We are going to Guthrie for supplies."

"You are welcome, you know that," Jed told him.

"Anna Marie know about this?" John asked.

"Nope," Jed sighed.

"Maybe we'll stop next time when the fireworks die down." John laughed a rich, full roar from the bottom of his chest, and rode away with his men.

"They talked just like us," Emma said in awe.

"What did you expect? War paint and a knife to scalp you with?" Jed asked testily. Less than an hour and he had to face the wrath of Anna Marie. It wasn't Emma's fault and he had no right to snap at her, but there was just so much a man should have to endure in one day. His sister's voice came back to haunt him like it had done for years when he least expected it. *That which does not kill us, makes us stronger,* she whispered in his ear.

Well, by tomorrow morning I should be strong as Samson just before he brought the walls down, he thought as he set the horses to walking again.

"Who is Anna Marie?" Emma finally asked.

"You want to talk about what you are running from?" he asked.

"No. I told you no awhile ago," she said icily.

"I don't want to talk about Anna Marie," he said just as coldly.

Emma clamped her full mouth tightly together. She drew her eyebrows down and swirled her lavender parasol around until it rested on her left shoulder, a barrier between her and Jed. Was Anna Marie his wife? Good grief, if he was already married, she'd really made a mess of her life. Then she remembered the sheriff saying something about all the women looking at Jed. Well, that was sure enough easy to believe. The man was so good-looking, especially when he grinned and that dimple in his cheek deepened.

She had to be his mother. That was the only other option. She was going to be really angry when he brought in a wife without even telling her about the wedding. Emma dreaded meeting the woman, but in only a few moments she could put his mother's mind at ease. She'd simply tell her about how chivalrous her son had behaved in keeping her out of jail. She'd let her know she was only staying two days and not to go to any bother.

"Your first wife dead?" Emma asked when the question popped into her mind. Surely, he'd been married to have four kids.

"Never been married before today," he said.

Talk about a tangled-up mess. Emma's brain went into overtime trying to figure out just how that happened. Anna Marie was his mother and he had four kids but he'd never been married. Maybe he had had an Indian woman living with him and producing children and when she died, his mother came to take care of the poor little orphans. They were probably kin to John Whitebear and that's why he asked if Anna Marie knew about the marriage.

Emma had read where folks frowned on that kind of thing even in Oklahoma, and the sheriff had said lots of women were looking at Jed. Well, they could look but that was all that had better get done. Their fathers and brothers would string him up for looking back at them. Jefferson Cummins would lay down in his cotton field and draw his last breath if he knew she'd married up with a man with four kids who were part Indian. She'd sure have a reputation now. Married to that kind of man and divorced from him too. No self-respecting man in the whole world would ever want her now.

"How much farther to your homestead?" she asked after they passed another mile of creek.

"Another hour," he said.

"What's that?" She pointed to the roof of a house set almost on the ground.

"That's a house. A dug-out. Folks haven't been able to put up a real home yet. Kind of like a cellar," he answered, but offered no more.

"You don't talk much, do you?" she asked.

"Not much to say," he answered. Yet, that wasn't the reason he wasn't talking and he knew it. There was lots to say. They were married for the next few months anyway. They could discuss what he expected out of her for room, board and saving her hide back in Guthrie. Having a woman at the place would be nice in some ways. The baby, Molly, wouldn't have to go to the field with him every day. He could get twice as much work done if he didn't have to stop and help the eldest, Sarah, cook supper. He and Jimmy could leave the women's work to the women. Emma was most likely educated, too, so she could help with homework.

If only it weren't for having to face Anna Marie, he might have adapted to the idea fairly well. Sleeping arrangements were going to be a bit of a problem. If he didn't spend the nights in the bedroom with Emma, the children would go to school and tell everyone that they didn't sleep together. He'd do the right thing and give her the bed and he'd roll up in a blanket on the floor. It was the only proper thing to do. After all, Emma didn't want to be married to him any more than he wanted to be married to her.

Before long, he might think about sending for cousin Beulah down in Texas. He didn't know why he hadn't thought of it before. Beulah was as round as she was tall and lost her husband with the cholera last year. She'd never had children but she was a jolly old gray-haired lady and she'd love to come to the homestead to help him.

"Is what you're running from illegal?" he asked as they rounded another bend in the creek.

"No," she answered bluntly, offering no more. She saw smoke rising from the chimney of a house nestling down in the rolling hills. So this was the homestead he talked about. It looked like a squatter's cabin but at least it was a real house, not one of those dug-out things they'd passed. The whole place was well kept; flowers blooming in the yard, split-rail fence around a couple of acres, long-horned cattle roaming in the pasture behind the house, and a few horses in the corral. But a far cry from the mansion in the middle of Crooked Oaks with its twelve white pillars holding up the balcony of the second floor. The balcony she'd stood on so many times as she'd looked out across the acres and acres of cotton fields.

"We're here." He drove the wagon through the yard gates, flung open by a snaggle-toothed little boy.

"You made it in time for supper." He noticed Emma and frowned. "Who is that?"

"That's not very mannerly, now is it, Jimmy?" Jed hopped down and ruffled his hair. "This is Emma."

"Hello, Emma. Sorry." He wiped his hand on the seat of his dun-colored britches stained with that infernal red earth before he held it out toward her.

She reached down and shook with him, surprised at how firm his small hands were. "I'm glad to meet you, Jimmy," she said.

Jed reached up for her, slipped his hands around her waist, and helped her down. Before she could blink, the front door burst open and girls in pigtails and gingham dresses poured out. Blond-haired little girls, with eyes ranging from light blue to deep green. They surely weren't half Indian children, but how could that be? How could he father four children without a wife?

"You're home! You're home!" The middle-sized girl

threw herself into Jed's arms and he swung her around. "Did you find a flour sack like the last one so I can make new pillow cases for my bed? Huh, did you? Who is that?" She stopped in the middle of her tirade as soon as Emma walked around the end of the wagon.

"Children, this is Emma. This is Sarah." Jed hugged the oldest child. "She's ten and my right arm around here. At least in the house. Jimmy is my right arm out in the barn."

"This is Mary. She's eight and no, I couldn't find a flour sack like the last one so you'll just have to have mismatched pillow cases. I don't think that will keep you out of heaven, though. We might ask Preacher Elgin about it on Sunday, if you're really worried," he said seriously.

"Oh, bother," Mary said. "What'd you bring Emma home for?"

"In a minute." He patted her head. "And this is Molly." He pulled a small girl from behind Sarah's dress tail. She had her thumb in her mouth and her forefinger crooked around her nose. She stared up at Emma with big blue eyes. Just like Jed Thomas's eyes. One thing for sure, he couldn't deny that child, no matter who their mother had been.

"Emma." She popped her thumb out of her mouth and reached up for Emma to pick her up. "Like Momma. Molly is going to like Emma."

"And Emma is going to like Molly," Emma said. The child cuddled down into Emma's shoulder like she planned to stay there forever.

"Jed, darlin', I wasn't expecting you for another hour at least. You're here early enough to sit down to supper with us." A short, dark-haired woman opened the front door, wiped her hands on the muslin apron she wore over a calico dress, and literally threw herself into Jed's arms. She tiptoed to kiss him on the cheek and then blushed when he didn't at least hug her back.

He held his arms stiffly to his sides. It wasn't proper for a married man to be hugging a woman other than his wife, not even if the marriage was only on paper. "Anna Marie,

I want you to meet Emma," Jed said, putting off using the word *wife* as long as he could.

Emma blushed red enough for both women. One who evidently was in love with Jed Thomas. The other who was his legal wife. One thing for sure, there was no way this petite woman was Jed's mother. She couldn't be a day more than nineteen.

"Emma?" Anna Marie held out her hand.

Emma readjusted her hold on Molly and held out her right hand. "Anna Marie. Pleased to meet you."

"Relative?" Anna Marie turned away to look Jed in the face.

"Let me take Emma's trunk inside. Then I think we'd better have a visit while I unload the chicken feed," he said.

"I think we'll have a visit right here," Anna Marie said bluntly. "Is Emma a relative? Is she a cousin? You didn't mention meeting anyone in town and bringing them home, Jed. You owe me an explanation and you better start talking right now."

He picked up the trunk and carried it to the middle of the front room floor and Anna Marie followed him, each question a little louder than the last one. Jimmy hung back at the edge of the wagon. Wasn't no way he was getting close to Anna Marie when she was mad. She'd thrown a plate at Jed a couple of weeks ago when he'd danced with Maggie more than one time at the spring dance over in Dodsworth. Sarah rolled her eyes and crossed her arms. So much for Anna Marie helping her with her math homework before she went home that evening. Mary followed them both in the house. She wasn't missing one bit of the fight and she fully well intended to tell the story at school. Too bad tomorrow was Saturday. Now she'd have to hold it all in until Monday. Molly just buried her face deeper into Emma's shoulder and began to howl.

"My Emma. It's my Emma and Jed can't take her back. Like Momma," she sobbed.

"Jed?" Anna Marie put her hands on her hips and waited just inside the door.

"Emma is my wife. We were married this afternoon by the justice of the peace in Guthrie," he said.

"Your wife?" Anna Marie screeched. "Your wife? I keep Molly all day and cook your supper and you bring a wife home, Jed Thomas? You scoundrel! I thought we had an understanding?"

"I never asked you to marry me, Anna Marie. I never even asked you to get engaged or not to see any other men," he said.

"No, but we both knew you would someday," she protested loudly. "I'm going home, Jed Thomas. I hope the devil gets your black soul." She picked up a cup from the table and threw it at him with enough force that when he caught it, it sounded like Molly's thumb when she popped it out of her mouth.

"You will live to regret this." Anna Marie shook her finger under Emma's nose as she stomped out to the barn to get her horse. "There's not a soul in the whole county who won't know about how you took another woman's man. And none of them will have a thing to do with you, you thief," she screamed as she rode off to the east.

"So that's Anna Marie?" Emma walked through the doors.

"Yes, it is. I think supper is about done. Looks like chicken and dumplings. You kids get your faces washed and we'll unload the wagon when we get finished eating," he said.

"Can I sit by my Emma?" Molly begged.

"Yes, you can." Emma set her on one of the benches on either side of a crudely built table. "I'll wash my hands and help." She followed Sarah to the washbasin under the pump beside the dry sink.

"Did you really marry her?" Jimmy whispered, drying

his hands while he watched Jed ladle up the dumplings from a cast-iron kettle on the back of the wood stove.

"Yes, I did," Jed said.

"I can't believe it." Jimmy shook his head.

"Neither can I," Jed answered.

Chapter Three

It was Jimmy's turn to offer up grace for the meal and he did so with very few words. Molly pulled her thumb out of her mouth before the "Amen" was hardly out of his mouth and the pop caused Jed to smile. He had a lovely smile. One that Emma might have liked if circumstances had been different.

Emma eyed the tiny house while Jimmy mumbled through his prayer. A living room, kitchen combination. A gorgeous black stove and a dry sink with a pump attached took up one end. The work table with rough shelves above it to hold dishes was on the south wall and the table on the other side of the room. Two backless benches held the four children, two on each side. Emma sat in a chair on one end, Jed at the other. A stone fireplace occupied the end of the living area side of the room. Two rocking chairs with patchwork cushion pillows in the seats were grouped with a sewing box between them. Braided rag rugs lay on the rough wood floor. A ladder was attached to the wall to the left of the fireplace and Emma could see beds up in the loft. That must be where the children slept. To the right of the fireplace was a treadle sewing machine, almost identical to the one she used at Crooked Oaks. A Singer that had been her birthday present last year from her father. Jed must occupy the room just off the living area. The door was open and Emma could see a white bedspread on a carefully made bed. White? In this red dirt world!

"I've got math homework and now Anna Marie is mad and gone home," Sarah said woefully. "Fractions, and we have to find common denominators and multiply and divide them. It's not due 'til Monday but I wanted to get it done so I don't have to think about it all weekend."

"I'll help you when we get the dishes finished," Emma said. "Now pass plates and I'll serve up these dumplings." Anything to keep her mind off that door leading into a room where she could see the white bed. She might be married, but she sure enough wasn't sleeping with Jed Thomas tonight or any other night.

"Yes, ma'am." Sarah held hers out first. Maybe having a woman around again wouldn't be so bad after all.

"Uncle Jed, did you check on the wood?" Jimmy asked.

Emma jerked her head around quickly but Jed didn't notice. Uncle? He was the children's uncle and not their father? She looked at each of them again when she helped their plates. Sarah, tall for her age, the same mossy green eyes as Jed. Mary, lighter green eyes and a dimple in her left cheek when she smiled, just like Jed. Jimmy, tall for his age, like Jed. And Molly, bless her baby heart, what had happened to their mother?

"Like Momma," Molly patted her arm as if she knew Emma's thoughts had been on her. "Like Momma. Emma can stay," she sighed.

"She misses Momma real bad," Mary said. "She don't usually take to anyone. Not even Anna Marie, but she likes you."

"Like Momma," Molly said again and reached her hands up to the sky.

"She means you're tall like Momma." Jimmy scooped up the dumplings and filled his mouth. "They ain't bad, Uncle Jed, but they sure ain't as light as the ones you make up."

"Oh?" Emma raised an eyebrow toward Jed.

"We got Joy's cook books and recipes she wrote up," he explained. "Joy was the kids' mother, my sister. Yes, Jimmy, I checked on the wood. This fall when things slow down we'll add another room or two to the cabin. We got lots of other things to think about first. Fields to get harrowed and cotton to get in the ground so we'll have a cash crop this year."

Recipes and adding additional rooms to the place were the last thing on Emma's mind. Was? Where was Joy now? Dead? Gone away forever, leaving these four precious children behind?

"Gone bye-bye," Molly said. "Emma's like Momma." Her blue eyes gleamed as she patted Emma on the leg, making sure she didn't go far away like her mother had done.

"You girls handle the kitchen and us menfolk will unload the rest of the wagon," Jed said. "I'll put your trunk in the bedroom." High color filled his cheeks as much as it did Emma's.

"Don't bother. I can get out what I need, and anyway tomorrow morning I would appreciate it if you would take me back to Guthrie."

"No!" Molly wailed. "No, Emma will stay. No, no, no." She shook her head violently, her braids making slapping sounds as they hit her cheeks. A sob caught in her chest and she gagged. Sarah jerked her up and made it to the front porch before the child threw up.

"Now look what you've done," Jed said coldly.

Emma threw down her fork and stomped out into the cool night air.

"If you weren't going to stay then why did you even come?" Sarah asked accusingly.

"Emma, my Emma," Molly's sobs broke Emma's heart in a jumble of jagged pieces. "Like Momma."

"Come here, baby." Emma took the baby in her arms and cradled her against her chest. "I'll stay for a while. Uncle Jed is probably too tired to make another trip into town so quickly anyway. Now you stop that crying and we'll all go in here and clean up the kitchen. I saw a sewing machine in the corner beside the fireplace. Does it work?"

"It was Momma's machine. It hasn't been used since she left," Sarah said, tears spilling down over her cheeks.

"Would it offend you if I used it?" Emma asked.

Sarah shook her head.

"Then tomorrow we shall make Molly a new dress to wear to church on Sunday," Emma said.

Sarah nodded. "I've still got homework."

"Then I guess we better get the dishes done and get busy," Emma said, trying her best not to think about the bed in that room.

"Emma will stay," Molly said between hiccups when they went back into the house. "I'm hungry."

"Then you can have another plate of dumplings while the girls and I get this kitchen cleaned up." Emma sat Molly on the bench and commenced to clearing the table. "I think you two men have business outside."

"Yes, ma'am," Jimmy said, smiling brightly. He and Jed had both heard the conversation on the porch. Jimmy held his breath until Emma said she'd stay. Jed would have gladly made the trip back to Guthrie. Talk about messing up a man's life with two words: *I do*.

"Come on, Uncle Jed. I'll help you put Emma's trunk in the bedroom and then we'll get that wagon unloaded." Jimmy grinned.

Lord, what had she gotten herself into, she let her eyes roll toward the rough beams of the ceiling. But the Almighty didn't send an answer floating down on the wings of an angel with a golden halo.

Fifteen minutes later Emma was helping Sarah with homework. Mary sat as close as she could get to her side and Molly snuggled down in her lap, sucking her thumb peacefully. "Okay, now this part is easy, divide the top by the bottom to get your percentage." Emma tapped the end of the chalk on the slate and gave thanks there wasn't a dozen little girls smothering her nearly to death.

"Oh, that is easy," Sarah said. "You should be a teacher, but Uncle Jed probably wouldn't want you to work. Not 'til Molly is older. Daddy always said a woman's place is in the home."

"And that's the right place," Jed said, coming through the door with Jimmy right behind him.

"Oh?" Emma raised an eyebrow. If she wanted to work, then she would work. No man, not even a husband, was going to shackle her to nothing but housework. She could do it all. Her mother, rest her soul in peace, had surely seen to that. If a woman was to run a successful plantation she had to know how to do everything. Once she had the knowledge it was perfectly acceptable to delegate the jobs to the hired help. But if she didn't have the know-how then the hired help could take advantage of her. Besides, even if she was a real wife, she could keep a house no bigger than this, teach school, and still have time to read Kate's novels.

"That's right," Jed said.

"Are you fighting on your wedding night?" Mary piped up with a sparkle in her eye. Boy oh boy, the story was getting better and better. She might even explode before she could get to school and tell it on Monday. She could tell part of it on Sunday after church but it would be so much better to keep it all for Monday when she could really be the queen in the center of a court of calico dresses and wide eyes.

"Of course not," Emma said sweetly. "Discussion is not fighting."

"Well, a bride is supposed to be pretty on her wedding night, ain't she Sarah? That's what Momma said when Anna Marie's sister got married up last year to that banker man. That's why Momma sewed up that fancy night rail for her. You got a fancy night rail in that big old trunk?" Mary tilted her chin to one side and grinned mischievously.

"What Emma has in that trunk is none of your business, you urchin." Jed's face was scarlet again. All these years he'd fancied himself a man's man and a knowledgeable source when it came to women, too. And in less than an hour the blond had him blushing twice.

"Well, all right, then," Mary said. "If you got your homework all done, Sarah, let's wash up and go to bed. You want us to carry you a pitcher of warm water to the bedroom and pour it in the basin, Emma? Ain't it romantic. Someday I'm going to be all grown up and it's going to be my wedding night." She sighed dramatically.

"And I'm going to come pester you all evening," Jed teased.

"No, you're not. Ain't nobody going to chivaree me neither like they did Minnie when she got married last month. I'm going to wash up and go to bed now," she declared by sniffing loudly and tossing her head back.

"Good night, Mary." Emma stifled a laugh. It could have been funny if it wasn't so scary. Just thinking about that bed gave her hives.

"Emma can sleep with me," Molly whispered.

"No, she can't," Jimmy said. "She's Uncle Jed's new bride and she's going to sleep with him. Right in there in Momma and Daddy's room. So come on Molly. You go up the ladder and I'll follow right behind you so you don't fall down. Oops, we forgot to take a pitcher of water in the bedroom for Emma."

"I'll take care of it, son." Jed cleared his throat and felt still another flush of heat traveling up his neck. "Good night, kids. We'll see you in the morning. Who wants pancakes for breakfast?"

"Me. I do. I do." Molly hopped around on one foot. "Good night my Emma." She wrapped her chubby arms around Emma's dress tail and hugged her tightly.

"Good night, my Molly," Emma smiled. It reached all the way to her eyes, and Jed forgot for a few minutes that she was so tall. Her face glowed with pleasure at the child's embrace. He wondered very briefly what it would take to make her glow like that for a man. He'd never know because she'd be gone in a few days. Until then he would be curled up on the hard wood floor with a pillow and a blanket. He almost moaned at how stiff he would be in the morning.

He went into the bedroom and appeared in just a moment carrying a crock pitcher. He used the long-handled dipper hanging on the wall and carefully filled it with warm water from the reservoir on the stove. He set it on the table and refilled the reservoir before he carried it to the bedroom and put it on the washstand beside the matching washbasin.

Emma sucked air deeply into her lungs, then exhaled slowly. What she should do was ask Jed very nicely to load her trunk on the wagon and let her drive back to Guthrie by moonlight. She could leave the wagon at the train station and he could retrieve it the next day. But Molly's face, all skewered up in a fit, haunted her. The child's mother must be dead. What kind of trauma would it do to her for Emma to disappear so quickly? Besides, if she was honest with herself, even Emma wasn't quite brave enough to face the night with no escort. No, she'd stay, for two more days. Come Monday morning, she'd be gone, though.

That was two days away. Tonight Emma had to go into that room, take her night clothing out of her trunk, and get ready for bed. Surely, Jed would be a gentleman. He didn't want to be married any more than she did, and he surely did not look at her like there was one thing about her that interested him. He was most likely cursing her under his breath for coming between him and his sweet Anna Marie. The devil woman with a tongue sharper than a two-edged sword. There was no understanding men. What on earth did he ever see in that shrew anyway?

"I'm surprised to see a stove so new in a cabin like this," she said, more to break the uncomfortable silence than anything else.

"Two things my sister insisted upon. Her stove and her sewing machine. Well, that and a whole wagonload of wood to build this cabin. It didn't have to be big or fancy. Just one room for the kitchen and living area. A little bedroom for her and my brother-in-law and a loft for the kids. That's what it took to get her to sell the family farm in Nebraska and come to the land run." Jed talked to cover his uneasiness.

"Well, she was a smart woman," Emma said. "Give me ten minutes and I'll have my night routine finished. Are you sleeping in the barn?"

"No, ma'am, I'm not," he whispered, pointing to the loft. "Little corn has big ears, you know. Mary is itching to get to school and tell this whole story. I think we better keep it simple; but don't worry. I'm not wanting to be married any more than you are, lady. It's just a marriage on paper. I will be a gentleman. Besides, you aren't my type, Emma."

She didn't know whether to drop down on her knees and give thanks or to slap fire out of his handsome face. She set her jaw and shut the bedroom door behind her. So she wasn't his type and he wasn't even the least bit interested in a big blond with rocks for brains. She had to be just what her father said—simple-minded—to have ever let herself get duped into this ruse anyway.

She poured the water into the basin and swished her hands around in it, enjoying the warmth. What she wouldn't give for a whole tub of warm water couldn't even be measured in money. To ease down in a steamy, hot bath and get all the kinks out of her muscles, tired from nights of sitting upright on a train bench. The floor didn't look too much better right then than the bench had, but that's where she would sleep tonight. She'd be strung up from the nearest pecan tree if she slept in that bed and made him take the floor. So she wasn't his type, she fumed as she unbuttoned her dress and let it puddle on the floor around her feet. She picked it up and draped it over the back of the rocking chair beside the washstand. She sorely missed her personal maid when it came time to undo the laces on her corset, but she managed to shimmy out of it and lay it on top of her dress. Next came the dainty, frilly camisole of the finest white cotton, trimmed in pink ribbons and lavishly pin tucked from top to bottom. And the matching drawers with lace ruffles and pink ribbons at the ankles. Stockings and shoes were last, and Emma stood there in nothing but what she'd come into the world wearing, twenty years before. She picked up the washrag and commenced to give herself a bath, enjoying even the small pleasure of being clean. When she finished she took the toweling hung on the rod across the fiddle back on the washstand and dried her whole body. She opened her trunk and took out a pair of clean drawers and a nightgown made of the same white cotton batiste. Pin tucks and tiny buttons, along with lace and aqua ribbons the same color as her eyes covered the front of the gown all the way to the top of a thickly gathered ten-inch ruffle around the bottom.

She took the pins from her blond hair and shook it down. It felt good to free her long, wavy hair from the tight bun on the back of her head. She didn't realize just how tired she was until she picked up her brush to give her hair the obligatory one hundred strokes. "One, what have I gotten myself into?" she counted aloud. "Two, has it been ten minutes? Three, the floor is beginning to look inviting. Four." A slight knock on the door and Jed cleared his throat on the other side.

"Yes?"

"Can I come in now?" he asked, barely above a whisper.

"Of course," she said. She could hear every fast heartbeat echoing in her ears. She hoped he just came in and fell into the bed. She didn't even care if he snored as long as he didn't want to claim her as a real wife. Or talk, either. The way her crazy heart was doing double time, she'd have a difficult time saying three words without running out of air.

He didn't know what to expect when he opened the door but Emma wasn't anything like he'd imagined. By the light of the coal oil lamp, she looked like an angel straight from heaven. Blond hair floating around her like a halo and a white robe just like he imagined angels wore. His mouth felt like it had just been swabbed out with a thick wad of cotton. If he'd had to spit or die, he would have just had to go on to meet his maker.

"I will take one of the quilts and a pillow and sleep on the floor," she said, amazed that she sounded almost normal.

"No, I will." He pulled his suspenders from his shoulders and let them drop. Just how much was he supposed to take off before her, even if she was just a wife on paper? Well, he might take the floor but he'd be hanged if he slept in all his clothing. His long underwear covered him up modestly. If that offended her, then she could take a pillow and blanket and head her own self right out to the barn, and to the devil with what Mary would tell about that.

"I insist." She threw back the covers on the bed to find a huge bolster on top of two pillows. "What's this?"

"Momma's bolster," Jed said. "Joy always liked it so she brought it with her when we came to Oklahoma. She said it made up a pretty bed to have the pillows and a bolster both."

"Hmmm." Emma looked at it. A bolster. A long, long pillow that stretched all the way across the bed. If it was only a little wider she could use it for a mattress on the floor.

"Joy was tall like you and Billy Trahorn was taller than me. He made this bed special. It's longer than most." Jed touched the headboard. Just thinking about how comfortable it was made him dread sleeping on the floor even more than ever.

"Jed Thomas, you are not my type, either," Emma said bluntly. "But we are married in the sight of God and witnesses. I do not intend to . . ." she began, blushing. "I do not intend to actually be a wife to you, but no one else will know that or ever believe it." She tossed the bolster in the middle of the bed, arranging it lengthwise to separate the bed into two separate units. "That's your side. This is mine. Do not cross the bolster with any part of your body and I will do the same. There is no sense in either of us sleeping on the floor. Now I'm tired and you promised the children pancakes for breakfast which I'm sure is very early. So let's go to sleep."

"Are you sure, Emma? I can sleep on the floor," he offered again but without a lot of conviction.

"I'm sure. Good night, Jed," she said just before she blew out the lamp. "I will shut my eyes until you are in bed so you don't have to be embarrassed."

"Thank you, Emma," he said softly and undressed quickly before crawling between the covers. It had surely been a day. Someday when he was old and gray he'd look back on it and laugh. But right then there wasn't one single funny thing about it.

She fidgeted with her pillow, turned over twice and finally noticed that her heart was still in her chest. It hadn't jumped out like it felt like it might do earlier. Jed really was going to be a gentleman and not demand his rights as a husband. There were a million questions in her mind, and no answers.

"So tell me about Joy and Billy," she finally said.

"Go to sleep, Emma. You'll be leaving soon. Two days? It won't matter then," he said, wishing he hadn't told her she wasn't his type. But blast it all anyway, she wasn't. He liked small women that fit under his arm just so. Women with big brown eyes and dark hair. Little red roses of women who needed his protective care and love. Not big, tall, yellow zinnias with eyes the color of sparkling creek water, who could fully well take care of themselves.

"I want to know," she insisted.

"Okay, okay," he said with a sigh. "Joy, Billy, and I came to the land run. We were better off than other folks because we had money and we'd done some planning. I staked a claim. Billy staked right beside me and Joy right behind him so we had three-fourths of a section."

"You mean women could claim land?" she asked incredulously.

"Yes, they did," he said. "We camped out with a couple of tents until the lumber got here. We'd already arranged to have it brought down from Kansas since we weren't sure how much would be available. Good thing, too. It was scarce in Guthrie. We put in a garden and built this cabin first thing. Then we put the barn up. I slept in a little room out in the barn. Then last winter the man who owned the other quarter of this section got cholera. He died and his wife caught it. Joy wouldn't listen, she had to go help the family. And she brought it home to Billy. They died within twenty-four hours of each other. We buried them up on a hill under a big spreading tree. The other man's wife lived and sold me their land before she took her kids back to Texas. It was a poor substitute for my two best friends. Now you know. Molly's been quiet and withdrawn until you arrived today. She'll be awful when you leave."

"I see." Emma's heart broke for him. She could hear the pain in his voice and the ache in his heart. She'd never had a sister or a brother so she couldn't imagine just how deep that hurt ran. She ached to reach across the bolster and at least pat his hand, but she couldn't make herself do it. She wasn't his type and he'd probably just throw her hand back in her own face. "I'm very sorry. Good night, again, Jed."

"Good night, Emma," he said.

"Good night, Jed." She turned over on her side, her back to her new husband. She watched the moonbeams dance through the window pane. Real glass windows out here in the territory. She wondered if that was another thing Joy had insisted upon. She shut her eyes tightly. Fatigue oozed from her body as she stretched her long frame out on the special bed, but sleep was a long time coming to Emma that night as she lay beside her new husband—who wasn't her type either.

Chapter Four

Jimmy stood just inside the door with a puzzled expression on his face. "Well, Uncle Jed?" he asked and blushed at the same time.

Jed raised an eyebrow but didn't slow down. He and Jimmy were going to work on clearing more land that day. They needed to check on the cattle that had strayed into the far reaches of his section of land, too. They had a knapsack full of leftover pancakes and sausage patties for lunch, along with a quart jar of coffee and one of well water. The girls were supposed to do their Saturday cleaning and have supper on the table when he and Jimmy got back home. A pot of beans was what he'd suggested, knowing that Sarah could well take care of that much. Emma seemed to know what she was doing when she'd taken over the breakfast, making pancakes and fried sausage that morning, but most likely she didn't know much past that.

Jimmy's face was still scarlet and he nodded toward

Emma, who wore a simple calico day dress that morning with one of Joy's bibbed aprons tied around her slim waist. Jed glanced back over his shoulder toward the stranger who was his new wife. She looked the same as she did yesterday, only a little more down to earth in that dress.

"Aren't you going to kiss her good-bye?" Jimmy whispered out the side of his mouth. "Daddy never left the house without kissin' Momma good-bye and ya'll just got married yesterday."

Jed's eyes widened as he nodded. "Well, we'll be getting along now. You have a wonderful day, Emma." He crossed the room in a few easy strides and kissed Emma quickly on the cheek. "Appearances," he whispered in her ear.

Her toes curled under. Her heart thumped around in her chest until she was sure the buttons on the front of her dress would pop right off. It just wasn't fair that a man's touch should affect her so. Especially one who only kissed her briefly on the cheek for appearances. She'd heard Jimmy whispering. It certainly didn't do her ego one bit of good for a man to brush his lips across her cheek because a small boy reminded him to do so.

"You have a nice day, too, Jed," she said, smiling. "Jimmy, don't you work too hard, honey. The girls and I'll have some supper ready when you get home."

Yeah, right, Jed thought. *Probably scorched beans and burnt cornbread. Bet she doesn't know one single thing about firing the stove. I just hope she doesn't burn down the house trying to show off. I'd rather she just left the beans to Sarah and spent the whole day picking wildflowers with Molly.*

"Okay girls," Emma said when Jed and Jimmy were out of the house. "What does cleaning the house on Saturday mean?" She looked around at the tiny little rooms. Her suite at Crooked Oaks was bigger than this whole house.

"It means we dust everything, take all the sheets off the beds and put the extra set on so they'll be clean tonight when we get our baths for church tomorrow morning. Then we pile all the dirty clothing in the corner in Momma's, I mean yours and Uncle Jed's bedroom, so it'll be ready on Monday morning for the washing. Uncle Jed and me and Mary try to get most of it done before we go to school on Monday but sometimes it has to wait 'til we get home. Then we put the clean sheets on and mop the floors and the porch when we get done. Uncle Jed said maybe beans would be all right for supper time, so I'll get a pot going when we get the dishes done," Sarah explained.

"Okay," Emma said. "Is that all there is? Just beans? Have we got a smoke house?"

"Yes, we still got a ham left from the butchering last winter. Uncle Jed's good with sugar and salt cure. And there's two slabs of bacon and a few rolls of sausage," Mary told her. "We got a spring house too, where we keep the butter and milk. I almost forgot, I need to churn what's ready and then we'll have almost two gallons of buttermilk."

"Come show me where the smoke house and spring house are." Emma dried her hands on the tail of her apron. "We'll have ham for supper. Ya'll got a root cellar?"

"We sure do." Sarah smiled brightly. "Got sweet potatoes, plain potatoes, beets, onions, and a few carrots left down there. Momma made a garden first thing when they claimed this here land. It was too late for green peas and I'm glad. I hate peas."

"So do I!" Emma smiled. "So Sarah, you are the upstairs maid while we go to the general store. Strip down the beds and dust whatever is up there. I'll do your Momma's, I mean mine and Jed's bedding. When we get back I'll help with the rest of the chores after we get the ham on to bake, and then we are going to make Molly a dress if we can find enough flour sacks," Emma said, planning the day as she followed Mary out the door.

"I'm going too." Molly grabbed Emma's hand.

"Good. You can help carry sweet potatoes," Emma said.

"Maybe we can take ham to the picnic tomorrow." Mary skipped along ahead of Emma.

"What picnic?" Emma asked.

"After church, we're having a social at the church in Dodsworth. We live closer to it than the one in Meridian so we go there. The church and schoolhouse are the same place. Got a bell. There's a little bitty store there but it don't sell as much as the big one in Guthrie does. Everyone brings their own lunch to the social and a quilt and it's kinda like the quilt is your house for the afternoon. We eat on our quilt and then the ladies all visit and the menfolk go talk about horses and plowing out under the two shade trees in the churchyard. It's the first one this year. We can't have them in the wintertime. Just when it's warm," Mary explained.

"I think ham would be nice for a picnic," Emma said. "And potato salad, and maybe even some ginger cakes if you've got ginger, and cinnamon in the house."

"Wow, you really are going to cook today," Mary said, grinning. "How are you going to sew and do all that, too?"

"I'll have lots of help," Emma told her.

"Here's the spring house. You need butter and milk for cooking?" Mary opened the door to a three-foot-square room, much smaller than the two-hole outhouse at the far end of the yard.

"Yes," Emma answered. The room was nice and cool, just like the one at Crooked Oaks, only much, much smaller. She picked up a square of butter and handed it to Mary, along with a half gallon jar of milk. She'd watched Jed strain the fresh milk that morning and send Jimmy out with two half gallon jars. The jar she picked up was chilled. She touched the ones at the back of the shelf and they were still warm. Yes, she'd chosen the right ones. "And some of this." She stacked a cube of lard on top of the butter, and was about to shut the door when she spied two very small squares of cake yeast laying on the shelf next to the rest of the lard. She picked it up and Mary giggled.

"Uncle Jed brought that stuff home for Anna Marie to see if she could learn to make bread with it. She got all huffy and said her biscuits was good enough for any man and she wasn't going to use that stuff. Momma used to make bread like that. I guess Uncle Jed kinda missed it. Momma kept something in the spring house after she made it so she could make more. I can't remember what it was called. I bet that stuff is all moldy and we'll have to throw it away," Mary said.

Emma picked it up and put it in the pocket of her apron. "It was called a sponge. Maybe it will still be good. We'll have to put it in scalded milk with some sugar and see if it bubbles. You take that stuff to the house and begin the downstairs dusting while Molly and I gather sweet potatoes and the ham. That the smoke house?" She pointed toward the west to a building that looked about the right size.

"Yep," Molly said. "Sweet 'tators are there," she said, pointing at a slanted cellar door. "Momma put them in there before she went far away."

They'd surely accomplished a lot in a few months. Even though it was small, they'd put up a house, built fences and a smoke house, had a butchering, dug a well. No one could ever say that Jed Thomas was a lazy man, that's for sure.

She found the ham hanging from a hook in the ceiling of the smoke house, took stock of the remainder of what was left of the last butchering. It would be a long time before frost when they could have pork again. Summertime was a time to live on whatever the land provided. Squirrel, deer, rabbits.

Joy hadn't wasted any precious time either, from the looks of the cellar. Bushel baskets held potatoes of both kinds, as well as beets and carrots. Shelves had been built around three walls and were filled with jars of fruits and vegetables. The rush wasn't held until April of last year, so they would have had to plow the ground and begin a garden immediately to get that many jars filled. Emma wondered how in the world they'd done it all with just three adults to work.

"Molly, where's the garden?" Emma asked when they were back out in the fresh morning sunshine.

Molly pointed to the other side of the house, where Emma saw minty green onion slips and rows of tiny green bean runners beginning to grow. The next year's growth was already in the making, and who was going to refill those jars in the cellar? Sarah was only ten years old and it wasn't fair to steal her childhood completely. All children should be encouraged to work and to learn, but they should have a little bit of time to be a child. Once she passed from a child into an adult, she could never go back and recapture the lost moments of just being a carefree little girl.

That wasn't Emma's concern. She was leaving tomorrow morning and Jed could go on raising his family the best way he could. Today though, she and the girls were going to have a good time. Making bread if the yeast hadn't died, and ginger cakes, and Molly a new Sunday dress, if there were enough feed sacks or flour sacks in the house that matched.

If. Such a tiny word that brought such big consequences. If she hadn't gone to the general store first. If she hadn't refused Matthew's offer and her father's demands. If, if, if. There was no going back, though.

"We're making ham for dinner and ginger cakes and Emma said potato salad for tomorrow at the picnic." Mary was dusting furiously when she opened the door, and talking to Sarah just as fast as she dusted.

"My, oh, my," Emma said. "Do you already have the upstairs done?"

"Yes, it's not very big. Not like our big old house in Nebraska. It had two floors and lots of rooms. The sheets are in the corner in your room. All us kids had our own bedrooms there. Someday when Uncle Jed gets time to build more rooms we will have here. Right now, we got a big bed for me and Mary and Molly to sleep in. Daddy hung up a sheet and Jimmy's bed is on the other side. Just a little cot bed like Uncle Jed has out in the barn. And I went ahead and took your sheets off too so your bed could air out like ours until after dinner. Then we'll put the clean set of sheets back on the beds." Sarah beamed. "Real potato salad. Oh, but we can't do that. Momma made mayonnaise and I don't know how."

"Well, I do," Emma said. "Now we'll save the mopping until after lunch. I mean, dinner. Here Molly, let me help you." She took the potatoes from the basket she'd made from the bottom of Molly's dress and noticed that her undergarments were in sad need of replacement. "Do you know where the flour sacks are?"

"Right here." Molly skipped across the room and opened the top of a roll-top steamer trunk beside the sewing machine. "Momma put the 'terial in here."

Emma squatted beside the trunk, amazed at what she saw. "Oh, my," she said, breathless with excitement.

"Momma was going to make us new dresses but . . ." Sarah's eyes teared up. "She bought those blue checks from the store in Guthrie and she always washed the flour sacks and feed sacks, too, then folded them up and put them in the trunk. The button box is right there and the machine 'tachments, too."

"Well, I guess we can make a new dress today," Emma said. "First though, let's get the stove stoked up and the ham in for dinner, I mean supper. Sarah, you wash the beans and put them on to cook. Make twice as many as usual and I'll make a quart of baked beans with the leftovers for the picnic tomorrow. Now about that mayonnaise. Mary, you can follow my directions. Molly, are you big enough to do the churn?"

"Can I?" Her eyes glistened. "Am I big enough now?"

"I think so," Emma said. "That can be your job and you can start right now. If you get tired we'll help out. Mary, where are the eggs?"

"There's six right here left over from breakfast," Mary

said. "You mean I can make mayonnaise? How many eggs do we need?"

"If you do just what I say, I bet you can. We need four so there's plenty. We'll need some more though for the rest of the cooking," Emma said. She put the ham in the dishpan and pumped cold water in on top of it. She picked up a clean dishcloth and began to scrub the ham vigorously. She'd need to bake it slowly, all day, maybe with a nice sweet glaze.

"Jimmy gathers eggs in the morning. They'll be in the spring house. Tell me how many." Mary grabbed a basket from a hook behind the stove.

"Let's think about it," Emma said. "None for the ginger cakes. Six for potato salad. Since we're making mayonnaise, we could boil some for deviled eggs to go with our picnic tomorrow, and for supper tonight, too." She giggled. She had used the word supper without even thinking about it.

Jed smelled the bread before he even opened the front door. The aroma filled the yard as well as the house. He hadn't had real yeast bread since before Joy died. Anna Marie refused to even try to make it, saying if her biscuits weren't light enough for him, then there were ten more fellows waiting at her back door just to get one. He wondered if she'd already opened the door and motioned for the first one to come on inside.

"What's that smell?" Jimmy untied his canvas nail apron and dropped it on the porch. "Smells almost like Momma's bread."

"I just hope it doesn't mean the beans have burned and fermented." Jed ruffled his hair. There wasn't any way the aroma was really fresh yeast bread.

The house was spotless clean; the girls were gathered around Emma on the floor while she read to them from the Bible. The whole scene would have made his heart swell if it had been Anna Marie reading to them, but the sight of

Emma sitting there in her nightgown with a shawl around her shoulders just plain made him mad. His heart was a lump of stone in his chest and his nose flared. Just as he thought. No bean pot on the back of the stove. Not even a pan of biscuits. She'd spent the whole day doing nothing.

"Uncle Jed!" Mary jumped up and ran to hug him. "I made mayonnaise. Emma told me just how to do it so we could have potato salad for tomorrow's picnic at church. You put the grease in one teaspoon at a time and beat and beat and beat."

"And I made butter," Molly said from Emma's feet. "Emma made me a new dress for tomorrow, too. And I picked out the buttons."

His mouth watered at the thought of potato salad. His sister made the very best he'd ever eaten. "You made butter, Molly?" he asked. Emma had set on her fanny all day and issued orders. The girls had made the butter and the mayonnaise. *She made a dress for the baby,* his conscience said bluntly.

Jimmy nudged him from behind. "You're supposed to kiss her when we come in. That's the way Daddy did it," he said, barely above a whisper.

"I see you've been busy." Jed bent to brush a quick kiss across her cheek. What he'd like to do was give her a piece of his mind for making the girls work so hard while she did nothing more than make a dress. *What you'd like to do is kiss her lips,* his heart said loud and clear.

"Yes, we have," Sarah piped up. "We got hungry so we went ahead and ate at supper time. Yours and Jimmy's is in the warmer. Wait 'til you see what we did. And the house is clean and we've already had our baths and Emma's got the water all ready for you and Jimmy in your room. Look, Uncle Jed, Emma even put our hair up in rag rollers so we can have curls for church tomorrow."

"I see." Jed touched Sarah's blond hair, all tied up in bits of cloth. "Well, you've always been the prettiest girls at church anyway, even with your braids."

"Look, Uncle Jed, ham and sweet potatoes and even baked beans," Jimmy said as he drew out a plate heavy laden with food from the warmer at the top of the stove. "Whoa, is it Christmas or what?"

Emma smiled. Jed seethed. Drat that woman anyway. Helping herself to his smokehouse and spring house. What could she be thinking? Making a meal like that on a plain old Saturday.

"What did you mean?" He turned on her, his green eyes dancing in pure rage. "I was saving that last ham for Anna Marie's birthday next week."

"Come on girls," Emma's aqua eyes bored into his with just as much anger. "We've read our love chapter in the Bible. Maybe your preacher will talk about that very thing tomorrow morning. Now I'll climb up the ladder and listen to your prayers. You two hungry men, enjoy your supper, and we'll discuss this later, Jed."

"Uncle Jed, that was just plain stupid," Jimmy whispered when he heard Molly doing her "God Blesses" in a loud voice up in the loft. "You married Emma, so you don't need the ham for Anna Marie's birthday. And look here what else I found when I checked the bread box for a biscuit. Real bread, like Momma made. I knew that's what I smelled."

"I guess it wasn't very smart of me," Jed said, wrinkling his brow. He picked up the knife and sliced off two slabs of bread. It was still warm and tasted like heaven when he bit into it. The sweet potatoes had been sliced open and sweet butter melted inside, then sprinkled with brown sugar. Ham had been cooked slow with a glaze, and the beans were done to perfection. So the woman could cook. She still didn't have any right to barge into his smoke house and do what she wanted without asking. Not even his real wife should take things upon herself without even considering that he might have other plans.

Jimmy took the first bath in the galvanized tub sitting in the bedroom. Before he climbed the ladder to the loft, he shyly kissed Emma on the forehead. "Good night, Emma. That was a fine supper," he said.

"Thank you, Jimmy," she said, forcing a smile to her face. She sat in the rocking chair, attempting to rock away her anger as she crocheted lace. She'd leave the lace in the roll-top steamer trunk along with the fabric and flour sacks and someday when Jed brought a real wife home, she'd put it on the bottom of new undergarments for the girls. That's as much as the new wife would get though. Emma would be shot graveyard dead before she left her recipe for mayonnaise or for ginger cakes either. Maybe Anna Marie could figure it out. After Jed's divorce was final.

Jed didn't say a single word about the supper she and the girls had worked so hard on, nor had he asked to see Molly's new dress. Maybe her father had been right all along. Marriage and love were two separate things. Love was that antsy feeling in the pit of her stomach when Jed kissed her. Or at least something like that, she surmised as she kept crocheting the picot-edged narrow lace. Marriage was simply a business proposition. She should have married Matthew and endured the part about making children.

Jed slipped down into the warm water and sighed. His muscles were tired. His brain was tired. If Anna Marie had made bread and a supper like what he'd just polished off he would have been profuse in his gratitude, but he couldn't make himself say a single word to Emma. Steam was still shooting out his ears when he thought about her just stepping in his house and taking over like a real wife would. Well, thank goodness she'd be gone on Monday and things could get back to normal around the homestead.

Emma finished the second piece of lace while she waited on Jed to finish his bath. She heard him sigh when he got into the tub. After a few sloshing sounds she could hear him padding around in the bedroom. High color filled her cheeks when she visualized him drying his body and putting on the fresh pair of long underwear that she'd laid on the top of the bed for him. She was fanning herself with the back of her hand to cool her burning cheeks when she heard the door open.

"I'll help you with that," she said, standing up and moving gracefully toward the bedroom where he was fighting with the oval galvanized tub. "The girls helped me carry out what we used." She talked in hopes that conversation would still her racing heart. Crazy thing, anyway. Jed didn't appeal to her. He wasn't her type and her heart could just wake up and realize that. Men by the dozens had courted her since she'd been old enough to wear long dresses and not a one of them affected her like Jed Thomas. But then she hadn't married any of them or slept in their bed, even with a bolster between them, either.

"Thank you," he said curtly.

They carried the water to the back stoop and across the yard to dump on the garden. Wasting water was next to sinning, according to what Sarah said when she'd been about to dump the water right off the side of the porch. Joy said even bath water could give the garden a drink, and in Oklahoma sometimes summers were long and hot. Sounded like Joy had a lot of common sense to Emma. Too bad her brother didn't inherit some of the same.

"Now, I'm going to bed," she said, turning her back on him and marching resolutely into the house. "Good night, Jed."

He found her curled up on her side, staring out the window at the stars and moon. He kicked his boots off and took up residence in his side of the bed. Two days before he could sprawl out all over the whole bed, and now he was relegated to only half. Not even that, if he considered the bolster which took up at least a portion of the center. He laced his hands behind his head and shut his eyes. But sleep wouldn't come, not until he made things right with Emma.

"I'm sorry about what I said about the ham and Anna Marie. It just slipped out," he said without looking at her. "And supper was very good. The bread was wonderful."

"Good night, Jed," she said, not trusting her voice to say another word. If this was the way husbands acted, she didn't ever want one. Hurt her feelings and make her bite her tongue to keep from crying and then try to make it all right with a few words. No thank you. She'd simply be that crazy old maid her father mentioned.

"I said I was sorry," he protested coldly.

"And I said good night," she said. "I promised Molly french toast for breakfast if you don't mind me getting into the sugar to make syrup. I used all the molasses in the baked beans."

"That will be fine," he said, all but gritting his teeth. "Good night, Emma."

She just sighed in response. One more night after this one and she'd be on the train bound for Enid, Oklahoma. She surely hoped there wasn't a sheriff waiting for her there, too. If there was, she'd go to jail before she married another worthless man.

Chapter Five

Molly held Emma's hand tightly as they walked into the frame building that served Dodsworth both as a church and a school. Emma held her head high and squared her shoulders as she stepped into the building. Mary and Sarah traipsed in behind her. Jed brought up the rear, right behind Jimmy since he'd held the door for them all. Emma slid into the rough wood pew and fully expected Mary to scoot right in next to her, but she didn't. She left a space wide enough for Jed, who managed to squeeze into the narrow place without so much as touching Emma.

He'd gotten a letter ready that morning while Emma primped with the girls' hair. After church he'd give it to Violet who would mail it for him the next morning. It was a summons for Cousin Beulah to please come to Oklahoma and help him at least through the summer months. Allowing for the time it would take to get the letter to her, and the time it would take for her to get things ready, he figured on at least three weeks before she could be there. After the picnic he intended to swallow a portion of his pride and ask Emma if she'd stay on and help until Beulah got there. He'd offer to pay her for her time and efforts, not that she needed the money. Anyone could tell by the dress she wore and the trunk she'd brought that she certainly did not need money.

"We are pleased to welcome Mrs. Jed Thomas into our midst," the preacher said. "We understand Jed has been holding out on us and got himself a mail-order bride much to our surprise."

Jed blushed. Emma blushed. Mary giggled. Sarah smiled. Jimmy grinned. Molly snuggled down deeper into Emma's lap.

"Now if you'll open your hymnals to song number twenty-nine, we'll sing 'Rock of Ages,' and then we'll ask Jed to lead us in prayer," he said.

Page turning created enough rustle to keep the people from staring awfully long at the tall beauty beside Jed Thomas that morning. Her burgundy skirt and pale pink blouse was of the latest creation, not to mention that hat. A pink straw with a froth of netting around the crown, tied up in the back with a bow centered a burgundy satin rose. Even her hat pins had pale pink heads on them.

Their voices blended together in harmony as they offered up praise to God in song. Molly sang the chorus as she pretended to read the words in the book Emma shared with Jed. When the hymn ended, Jed stood up and offered thanksgiving for the beautiful day and the opportunity to meet with faithful Christian folks. He didn't offer up public thanks for a new wife, but then Emma figured that was for the best. One day of uttering lying vows before the Almighty was testing their luck. Two would be downright disastrous.

The preacher spoke from Corinthians 15 about love and what it would accomplish in anyone's life. The message was beautiful. Anna Marie's glares let Emma know right quick that she wasn't listening to a single word the preacher said. "And now, in closing, I want to announce the engagement of our youngest daughter, Sally, to the blacksmith over in Guthrie. She'll be moving over there at the end of this school year and our community will be in sore need of a new teacher. Anna Marie might have to pick up the reigns if we can't find one. Now, we'll ask Sally's intended to offer up our benediction."

The young man stuttered and stammered over a prayer and Emma heard Jimmy sigh when it was done. Evidently he'd been thinking more about running and playing with other boys his age than all those words about love in our hearts. The minute the future groom uttered "Amen," Jimmy jumped up and headed for the door.

Molly followed her two older sisters outside, and Emma brushed the wrinkles from the front of her skirt where Molly had been sitting. Jed waited patiently, playing the perfect new groom part well. He'd have to work hard not to offend her if he really wanted her to stay around and help with the kids for a while. The idea had come to him sometime after she'd gone to sleep the night before. She wouldn't ever make a wife he could really love or even tolerate on a long-term basis, but she might make a good hired hand. Take care of the cooking and maybe even make a few dresses for the girls. Goodness only knew Jimmy could use a few new shirts, too. And after a couple of nights of sleeping with her and the bolster, well, that wasn't so bad either. Half a bed wasn't any worse than his small cot out in the tack room and at least she didn't snore or talk in her sleep. He could manage his part quite easily since she wasn't the type of woman he could really love.

Introductions had to be taken care of and he did them so well, with his hand on the small of her back, burning holes through her bow Basque jacket, which was suddenly too hot for the warm morning. She smiled sweetly, told everyone she was pleased to meet them in her softest most southern voice. Everyone, that is, except Anna Marie, who drew her eyes down at Emma for a split second before she turned on the charm to Jed.

"Why, good mornin' Jed, darlin'. I didn't know if you'd be in church this mornin' or not. Didn't know if you could face Daddy after that sneaky little stunt you pulled. But I do want you to know that I have forgiven you. Let bygones be bygones. Oh, by the way, I thought you might like to know that Mr. Alford Manor will be at the picnic this afternoon. He's coming special to see me. He's the banker over in Guthrie. So don't you worry your little heart none about upsetting me. Alford has been asking for simply weeks for Daddy's permission to court me. Have a good day, now Jed. And if you need to visit our quilt to get some kind of decent food, please feel free to do so," she said, sniffing loudly as she shoved her nose into the air.

"Well, darlin' Jed, shall we go see if you can choke down my lunch, I mean dinner? I suppose you could go visiting if you can't. And who is her daddy? Someone I need to be afraid of?" Emma asked.

"Her father is the preacher," Jed said. His voice was cold as clabber as he steered her out the door and onto the lawn where the kids had the blanket spread on a grassy spot just barely under the shade of a huge pecan tree. Jimmy was toting a jar of coffee and one of cold tea. Sarah had the picnic basket, complete with plates and forks. Mary carried two jars of potato salad and Molly had a smaller basket filled with ginger cakes.

"So that's why he preached on love this mornin'." Emma spread her skirt out in a fan around her legs and sat down gracefully. "You've sinned against his daughter and you need to repent."

"I did not," Jed protested. "I never had an agreement with Anna Marie."

"But you wish you had, don't you? Then you wouldn't be in the mess you are in today," Emma said. "Jimmy, honey, please go fetch that other basket. It's got the beans and napkins in it. I'll begin to help your plate while you are gone so that you can gobble it all down and go play with your friends."

"Thanks, Emma." He was off and running toward the wagon in one leap.

"I don't know what I wish right now. I guess that you'd hurry up and get Jimmy's plate done so I can be next. I'm starving," Jed said. Yes, he did wish he had proposed to Anna Marie. If he'd been engaged he wouldn't have told the sheriff he was going to marry Emma. Anna Marie would have grown up someday and made a wonderful wife. She would have lost that temper streak and learned to make wonderful bread. She would have produced lots of sons for him and they would have had a long happy life on the homestead. But he sure wasn't going to tell Emma that right now. Not when he wanted her to stay around until Beulah could get there. Lord, the thought of the tantrum Molly would throw was enough to make the hair on his neck stand right up and tingle. If Beulah was there, it wouldn't be so bad.

"Okay, don't answer me," Emma said, helping his plate with a big slab of glazed ham, potato salad and beans Jimmy handed her. She added a thick slice of her home-made bread and three deviled eggs. "Now if you can't choke that down, you just chase right on over there to that wedding ring quilt Anna is sitting on with her sister, and have some of their fried chicken." She nodded in the direction of the Elgin girls and their parents sitting under the other shade tree.

"I think this will do fine," Jed said. If he didn't know better he'd think maybe Emma was jealous. Women! Couldn't live with them and it was against the law to shoot them. At least that's what his grandpa used to tell him when he was a little kid, and it was sure enough beginning to make sense.

"How's the potato salad, Uncle Jed?" Mary asked. "Is the mayonnaise as good as Momma made? Emma said I had to beat it and beat it, after every teaspoon. And I did.

Emma said it was very good, that she couldn't do better if she'd made it."

"It's wonderful, Mary." Jed shoved another spoonful in his mouth and it was indeed as good as the bread. Almost, anyway.

"Hello, Jed." A tall woman looked down at the family. "Mind if I join your quilt since I'm all alone and didn't bring one? I did bring a sandwich." She held up a tin lard can like the children carried their lunch to school in.

"Violet McDonald, meet my new wife, Emma. Emma, this is the local seamstress and wife of Zeb, who works for the railroad and is gone quite a lot," Jed said.

"Please join us, Mrs. McDonald." Emma made a place for her. "We've got a couple of extra plates and forks and plenty of food so put your sandwich away. We'd love to share our dinner with you."

"Well, you don't have to twist my arm. That potato salad looks scrumptious and I haven't glazed a ham in forever. You must have been a busy woman yesterday, and the day after your wedding at that." Violet took the plate from Emma's fingers and began to eat.

"And she made Molly a new dress too," Sarah said. "Us girls all helped get things done. Whatever Emma said. And she sewed and cooked and cleaned with us. Look at Molly's new dress. She even tucked the front of it and crocheted some lace for the collar."

"You sew?" Violet eyed the lady closer. At first glance she figured Emma for one of those southern ladies who'd never done a single thing in her life. That's the way she appeared with that fancy skirt and newest in fashion bow Basque jacket. No one in Guthrie had one of those yet. Not until Violet had time to send for a pattern and make some to sell in the dress shop over there.

"A little," Emma said modestly.

Violet studied Molly's dress in detail. Pin tucks as straight as a sober judge. Keyhole button holes and true to Sarah's word, really dainty crocheted lace around the collar. Fine lace, size 11 crochet hook and the thinnest thread with picot edging. "Nice work. Use Joy's machine to do that?"

"Yes, I was glad to see a good sewing machine. Family model Singer. My dressmaker at home uses the medium one. It's got a longer arm but basically is the same. Daddy gave me the family model for my birthday last year," Emma said.

All Jed caught was the fact that she had a dressmaker wherever she came from. Everything about Emma contradicted itself. She carried herself like gentry, but the rich folks didn't know how to cook and sew like she did. She spoke of a dressmaker, but if she did come from the well-to-do, then what was she doing in Oklahoma?

"I could sure enough use someone with your talents," Violet said. "I make things and take them over to the dress shop in Guthrie once a week on Tuesdays when I pick up Zeb at the station. He's home on Tuesdays, Wednesdays, and Thursdays. I'll supply the materials if you'll make some little girl dresses in your spare time. Pay you a little, too."

"Thanks, but no thanks," Jed said. "My wife doesn't need to work. I can support us."

Every nerve ending in Emma's body rose up in protest. How dare he say what she could and could not do? How embarrassing for her not to be able to make her own decisions. After all, their marriage was on paper, not in their hearts. She'd be gone tomorrow but he still didn't need to make her decisions.

"Jed, darlin', have some ginger cakes. They're an old southern recipe right from my own grandmother's cookbook. They're more like cookies than cakes and the longer they sit, the better they get. Momma used to say if we could leave them alone for six months they'd be aged perfectly, but it never happened." Emma ignored his comments. "You too, Mrs. McDonald. When you finish your dinner, the ginger cakes are in this little basket. Jimmy, you take an extra couple for your little friends. There's plenty. The recipe makes four big pans full."

"Don't call me Mrs. McDonald. I'm only twenty-five years old. Call me Violet. I think we might be friends, Emma Thomas." Violet grinned.

Jed felt like he was the only rat at a tomcat party for some reason. He'd just made a comment about Emma not sewing or making money. Before he could blink twice the conversation turned around and the two women were acting like he wasn't even on the face of the earth. He'd show them. He didn't have to put up with being ignored. "I'm going over to visit with Preacher Elgin about my bill for the kids' schooling. I'm leaving you in good hands, Emma. Violet will make you at home with the rest of the women-folk."

"I'm sure she will, Jed, darlin'." She drew out the darlin' in true southern form.

"Now that he's off in a snit, will you sew for me?" Violet asked again.

Anna Marie ignored Jed while he talked to her father. She crossed the churchyard and plopped down beside Emma without an invitation. "Not bad," she said, biting into a ginger cake from the basket. "Suppose Sarah found the recipe in her mother's things. Jed won't ever keep you, you know. He's always been in love with me. Ever since that first day when we raised the church house and the whole county came to help. He'll kick you out one of these days. Of course, I'll be married to Alford by then and he'll just have to go to his grave knowing he made a big mistake in marrying someone as big and ugly as you are. Good cookies. Good-bye now."

"Wait just a minute, Anna," Emma stood up to her full five feet eleven inches and towered above Anna. "I don't think Jed will kick me out. He's real partial to my hot bread as well as other things I do that make him feel like a king. Honey, don't you worry about him going to his grave think-ing he made a mistake. We'll be sitting on the front porch of his house when we're both old and gray, watching our grandchildren play in the front yard."

"You are crazy as well as ugly," Anna Marie whispered hatefully and stomped off to join a group of young women sitting on the church steps.

"That Anna Marie. She's a handful. I don't envy any man who gets her. Don't pay any attention to the wench. Jed's better off without her. So are you going to sew for me?" Violet asked again.

"Of course I am," Emma smiled. She wasn't leaving tomorrow morning after all. Jed could just get used to the fact she would be around for a while. Wasn't no way in the green earth she was going to let that wench win this catfight. No, she'd stay around for a few weeks. Get the girls some dresses made and maybe even Jimmy a few shirts. The steamer trunk had enough fabric in it to do lots of sewing. And she would sew for Violet, too. One thing she'd discovered long ago when her mother first set about to teach her to operate a treadle sewing machine, is that she could fairly well make the machinery hum. Maybe it was because she was so tall and had good long feet to make the pedal go fast. "You bring me the stuff tomorrow and I'll start work on it in the evenings. I figure I can do four dresses a week and still get these kids' things made, too. Instead of money for the first four, could you please get me a bolt of nice white cotton and some pink ribbons? The girls are in dire need of new drawers and camisoles and Sarah wants a real petticoat in the worst way."

"I'll do it," Violet said. "You going to handle Jed on this or do you want me to talk to him?"

"I can handle my own sweet husband," Emma said with a smile. "Any particular style of little girl dresses you want?"

"You just make 'em, and I'm sure they'll sell like hotcakes," Violet answered. She already liked Emma. Poor old Jed didn't know he'd married a smart woman as well as a real beauty. Anna Marie was simply green with jealousy.

Not as much for losing Jed because men were thicker than fleas on a mangy dog in the territory, but because Emma was simply the lady she would never be. "These really are good ginger cookies. Do they keep forever like you said, and do you give away recipes?"

"Yes, and yes. I'll write it off for you and have it ready when you bring the fabric tomorrow. I could take it with me today," Emma offered.

"No, give you a day to fight it out with Jed. Remember, the bigger the fight the better the making up. Sometimes I start a good fight with Zeb just so's we can go to the bedroom and make up," she said, giggling.

"Ain't it the truth," Emma joined her. Talk about lying vows. She was sure going to have a lot to account for on the judgment day.

They lay side by side with nothing more than the bolster and heavy silence separating them. She had to tell him she was staying on for a while to make the children some clothing. She wouldn't mention Anna Marie's hateful remarks. He didn't need to hear the love of his life saying the words he already felt in his own heart. The homestead was a wonderful hiding place anyway. There was no way Jefferson Cummins would ever find her here in this backwater existence. He'd be looking for her in fancy boarding houses in big towns like Guthrie. Maybe God had sent a blessing when she ran into Jed Thomas in the general store after all.

Jed laced his hands behind his head and tried to figure out a way to say his piece to Emma. She was all set to go the next day. He didn't have time to take her to town and he sure didn't want to be the laughingstock of Logan County when word got round he couldn't keep a mail-order bride but two days. One that could cook like a chef, sew like a professional, and make bread to boot. If she only had dark hair and came up to his shoulder. He sighed. Not one time in the months when he'd kissed Anna Marie had his heart beat so fast as when he simply touched his lips to Emma's cheek. But it was Anna Marie he wanted.

"I liked Violet," Emma said.

"Uh-huh," he muttered.

"What state did she come from?"

"Texas, which reminds me," Jed said. "I sent a letter to Guthrie with Violet today. I've got a cousin in Texas who's recently been widowed. She's fifty if she's a day and I've asked her to come help me with the children. I figure I'll have an answer back in about three weeks. Four at the most. Anyway, I would like to ask you to stay on that long. I'd be willing to pay you for your time and trouble. The kids get along well with you and Molly doesn't need another heartbreak so quick." There, he'd done it. It hadn't tongue-tied him or hurt his pride either. He'd just spit it out like a man and now she could say yea or nay.

"You'd pay me?" She wanted to hug herself.

"Of course," he said.

"Good, because I want pay. Only I don't want money, Jed. I want to make dresses for Violet. That's the only way I'll stay. If you agree not to fight with me about sewing. She's going to buy me a bolt of white cotton with my first week's dresses so I can make the girls some decent underclothing." She was glad it was dark and he couldn't see her face when she talked about unmentionables. She almost giggled at that thought. She was a married woman, and she had trouble talking to her husband about underclothing.

"I can buy whatever the girls need," he said tensely.

"You're right. You can buy the fabric and pay Violet to make them or I can do it with my earnings. It's my condition to stay here and help you. It's pretty slim pay for three or four weeks' work around here, if you ask me," she said.

"I'll pay you honest wages," he said through clenched teeth.

"I don't want honest wages. I want to be able to make a decision on my own," she said.

"Next thing you know you'll be wanting to vote, too," he snapped.

"Sounds good to me. You fix Congress so I can vote and I might stay six weeks. Have we got a deal, Jed?"

"We've got a deal, Emma, even if I don't like it," he said.

"Then good night, Jed. One more thing, since I'm staying awhile, do I have to make everything right with you before I raid the smoke house or the cellar again? Do you have something else put up for Anna Marie's birthday?"

"You can cook whatever you can find," he said. "And there'll be no more talk of Anna Marie."

"Thank you, Jed," she said. She turned her back to him and smiled even brighter than the stars twinkling in the window.

Chapter Six

Emma had just finished hanging the last load of clothes on the line when Violet drove her buggy into the yard. She and Molly met her on the front porch and invited her inside for a cup of tea.

"Only a short cup," Violet said. "I brought fabric for ten dresses. You do them whenever you get time. No hurry. I'm going in to get Zeb tomorrow morning. I'll pick up the cotton you asked for. On Sunday you can bring whatever you got done and I'll have your bolt wrapped. We'll just slip them into the back of our wagons without much fuss. Preacher Elgin might look down on us for doing even that much business on Sunday. So how did you make out with that good lookin' husband of yours?"

Emma set the tea kettle on the back burner and pulled down three cups from the shelf above the dry sink. "Oh, it was easy. We made a deal."

"I just bet you did and from the color in your cheeks, I

won't even ask what kind of deal it was," Violet chuckled. "I bet by the time the deal is worked out Anna Marie won't have a leg to stand on either. Don't let that wench's hateful words upset you, Emma."

"They don't," Emma said. "I just consider the source. If I had my claws into something as handsome as Jed, I'd get pretty mad if someone declawed me in my sleep. She's got a right to be angry, don't you think?"

"Probably," Violet agreed. "But Jed's a better man without her. She's gone over to Guthrie to stay with her married sister a few days. No doubt, she's got that Alford man in her sights now. Bless his heart."

"He's going to need it," Emma said. "Poor man doesn't know how much. What was the good Lord thinkin' of to give someone like her to a preacher man?"

"Our Father who art in Heaven doth have a sense of humor, evidently. There's the kettle. Just pour me half a cup of hot water and slip the tea in. I'll finish filling it with cold water so I can drink it quickly and get on home. I've got the trim to put on three dresses so they'll be ready to take tomorrow. Can't keep them sewed up fast enough," she said.

Molly and Emma stood on the porch and waved until Violet was completely out of sight. The clothes were flapping in the morning breeze, the house was clean and straight. Jed said he'd be close enough to come in for lunch and Emma had a pot of beans boiling on the back of the stove with the ham bone in them for seasoning. She'd pan-fry a skillet of potatoes with slivers of onion and slice off a healthy chunk of the last loaf of bread for his lunch. Then they could eat the leftovers for supper. Maybe she'd get a jar of peaches from the cellar and make a cobbler to round it out. But first she was going to cut out one of the dresses and get the most of it sewed up. If she had it finished to the handwork, she could do that tonight after supper while she played overseer on the kids' homework.

"Come on, Molly," she said. "You can sit on the floor and pick out buttons for me."

"I can get them all out of the box and make them match." Molly nodded seriously. "Is this a dress for another little girl?"

"Yes, it is. And next week I'm going to sew you up some brand-new underclothing," Emma hugged her tightly.

"With lace and pink ribbons like yours?" Molly asked, remembering the pretty things hanging on the clothesline beside Uncle Jed's long underwear.

"Yes, with lace and pink ribbons," Emma smiled.

Before they could open the door, a big overgrown dog came bounding around the house. He stopped at the porch, his hackles raised and a deep growl in his throat. He approached them slowly, a step at a time. It wasn't a spider so Emma couldn't very well squash it. She eased Molly behind her and whispered to the child to get into the house in a hurry.

"Why?" Molly asked.

"Because I said so," Emma whispered again.

"Are you afraid of Buster?" Molly asked.

"Who?"

"Buster?" Molly said and ran out into the yard before Emma could stop her. "Buster, come here Buster," she giggled as she grabbed the dog around the neck. "See, he won't hurt me. But he don't like nobody but us and Jed. He hates Anna Marie."

"Oh, he does?" Emma asked.

"Yes, come on Buster, Molly will put you back in your pen. Did Jed leave the door open?" Molly pulled on him, dragging him by one ear back around the house.

When the dog saw the clothes flapping in the wind, he shook loose from Molly's grasp on his ear and chased over to tug on a pair of Jed's underwear. Emma came off the porch quicker than a bolt of lightning. "You miserable mutt, don't you dare touch my laundry. I'll jerk your ears off your big old black head and feed them to the hogs," she said, grabbing the dog by the same ear Molly had just moments before.

The dog wagged his tail and turned his head to lick her arm. "And don't you lick me either. Yuk, you got a mouth as big as a bull."

Molly slapped her hand over her mouth and giggled. "Buster likes you, Emma. Buster was Momma's dog and he don't like Anna Marie but he likes you."

"Well, we better be taking Buster back to wherever Jed keeps him," Emma said. "Where is that, Molly?"

"Buster has to stay in the pen when we do laundry. Momma used to get the broom after him 'til Uncle Jed made the pen. Had to make him stay in it when Anna Marie came, too. He really don't like her." Molly got the other ear and the big horse of a dog followed along like he was going to heaven.

"He's dug out from under the fencing," Emma said. "It won't do a bit of good to put him in there. Come on you mongrel, I'll tie you to the front porch post, and you better not even think about chewing the rope. Molly, run in the house and get me that length of clothesline beside the door. The one Jed used to tie stuff down on the wagon."

Molly took off in a galloping run typical of three-year-old little girls and Emma put her arms around the dog's neck to keep him from getting away. Buster wagged his tail and whimpered. His lady friend had come home. The one who'd been gone for so long. She always yelled at him when he tried to take those crazy flapping things from the clothesline so he knew it was her. Besides she was tall like his friend and smelled just like her.

"I got it," Molly sing-songed as she came around the house.

"We'll tie it around his neck like this," Emma said as she worked. "And we'll lead the big old bruiser to the front porch like this and tie him up."

Buster bounded toward Emma until he reached the end of his rope, then he laid down and whimpered, his big black eyes begging her for attention. "Oh, you big mean baby," she said, bending down to scratch his ears. "I've got sewing to do. We'll play when there's no laundry on the line and Molly and I don't have work to take care of."

At noon, Jed stormed through the front door, his face ashen and his eyes wide. "Molly, how did Buster get tied up to the porch post? Did he hurt Emma?"

"No, he didn't hurt me." Emma appeared out of the bedroom where she'd been straightening her hair for dinner. "Seems to like me, the crazy thing. Growled at me until we had a fight over the clothes on the line, then he just whimpers and begs me to scratch his ears."

"Well, I'll be hanged." Jed sat down with a plop. "He hates women. Since Joy died he's been so cantankerous, I thought about giving him away."

"No!" Molly screamed. "Not Buster. Don't give Buster away. He's going to be good now."

"That's right." Emma picked her up and set her on the bench in front of the big kitchen table. "He'll be good. Come say grace, Jed, so we can eat. I'll get it on the table while you wash up."

Jed could scarcely believe his eyes or ears. A good hot dinner with Buster tied to the front porch by Emma. *You always remember to trust the instincts of a dog or a child,* his grandfather's voice came back to haunt him. *I never did say I didn't trust either one, just that I wasn't about to marry a woman as tall as me and as stubborn as a Missouri mule,* he argued right back.

"Now, Molly, I will help your plate," Emma said.

"Lots of fried potatoes. Molly likes fried potatoes," she said.

"So does Emma," Emma laughed. A rich full laugh from her chest that made Jed sit up straighter and take notice. Women he knew didn't laugh like that. They put their hand over their mouth and giggled. Emma's laughter sounded natural and right and he liked it. But that didn't mean he could tolerate the woman for more than three weeks. The sewing machine was covered with pieces of something she was making. Most likely for Violet because he'd seen her driving her buggy back toward Dodsworth.

"Does Uncle Jed like fried 'tators?" Molly asked, wanting to keep the high spirits rolling.

"Of course he does, sweetheart." Jed scooped several spoonfuls onto his plate. "It's a treat for us to have a good hot dinner, isn't it Molly?"

"Well thank you." Emma cocked her head off to one side and smiled.

"Thank you." Jed looked deeply into those strange aqua-colored eyes. In a moment he cleared his throat and dropped his gaze to the plate of food in front of him.

Men! she thought. *Fix him a ham and all the trimmings and he gets so mad he could lay down and die. Make him red beans with the ham bone and some fried potatoes and he thanks me. Talk about it being hard to understand women. They are like understanding the makings of a locomotive compared to understanding the mind of a man.*

"Emma is going to make me new underdrawers next week with ribbons and lace like hers," Molly said between bites.

Jed blushed again. He'd noticed the delicate things hanging on the clothesline when he ambled in from the field he'd been plowing all morning. Just seeing them there had made his mouth go dry like it did every night when Emma crawled into bed wearing that angelic-looking nightgown.

"Tell me about your morning." Emma changed the subject quickly.

"Nothing to tell," Jed said. "Plow, plow, and more plow. Getting the field ready to sow alfalfa to make hay for the winter so the cattle won't starve this winter. And cotton so we can have a selling crop for money to survive."

"I see. It is about time to get the cotton in the ground, isn't it?" she said.

"You come from cotton-growing folks?" he asked.

"Yes, I do, but I don't want to talk about it," she said.

"Why?" Molly asked.

"I just don't. Tell Jed about picking out buttons for me, okay?" She steered Molly's mind to something else so quickly, the child didn't even remember the question.

After four ginger cake squares and a cup of hot coffee, Jed went back to the field, whistling. This arrangement wasn't so bad after all. He'd gotten twice as much work done that morning than when he had to be constantly watching after Molly. His stomach was full of good hot food and Buster could even be turned loose once the clothes were off the line. Maybe Buster would even like Cousin Beulah and things could just continue right on going well. He'd give her the bedroom and he'd move back to the barn into his old tack room. Yes, siree, things were really looking good.

The kids came in from school hungry as young coyotes and twice as active. Emma sent Jimmy to do his outside chores, Sarah to setting the table for supper and Mary to peeling more potatoes. She hoped the new crop in the garden was ready before the ones in the cellar ran out. If she continued using them for two meals a day, they might not last that long. Maybe she'd ask Violet to pick up a sack of rice next time she was in Guthrie. That would help stretch the potatoes until harvest time.

She finished the dress she was making and laid it aside for the hand work later. She'd hem it, tuck all the facings in with blind stitches, and crochet a bit of lace around the collar and perhaps on the edge of the armband if she had time. She'd washed her hands and was about to put a pan of corn bread into the oven when Mary finished the potatoes and said she'd run down the cellar for an onion to fry with them.

"That would be nice," Emma said. "By the time you get back I'll have the grease hot and the potatoes sliced."

Emma heard Mary giggling and Jimmy fussing but didn't pay any attention until Jimmy's voice came through the window, loud and clear. "I'm getting Uncle Jed. You know better, Mary Trahorn."

That's when Emma stepped out on the back stoop and saw Mary on the edge of the well, both hands out holding an onion in each one and walking around the edge. One misstep and the child would tumble many feet down into a dark, deep well. Emma held her breath and made herself not scream for fear she would startle Mary and make her fall. Although her knees were filled with jelly, she walked carefully to the well until she was behind Mary and deftly picked her off the housing with one arm.

"What?" Mary screamed. "Put me down right now."

"I will not." Emma toted her inside the house as if she was no more than a sack of flour. "You know better than to pull a stunt like that Mary, and you are going to be punished for it. So shut your screaming and accept it."

"You can't punish me. You're not my mother," Mary screamed even louder.

"No, I'm your aunt and I'm helping raise you, and you will mind me." Emma carried her inside the back door and pulled the rocking chair around to face the corner with one hand, still holding tight to Mary with the other. She plopped her down hard enough in the chair to cause a thud. "You will sit right there and think about the scare you gave me until supper time."

"I will not." Mary started to hop up, her bottom stinging from the impact of being thumped down so hard in the chair.

Emma put her hand on Mary's shoulder and forced her back into the chair. "Yes, you will. And you won't talk either. You will think about your silly deed and we will talk about it later."

Sarah's eyes bugged out and Molly had her thumb in her mouth, sucking for all it was worth. Jimmy watched from the back door, shaking his head and wondering what Uncle Jed would think of that. He'd told Mary two times last week to stay off that well. One thing for sure, he wasn't going to be happy about her being on it again.

Emma's chest hurt from holding her breath. That child would be the absolute death of her in three weeks' time if she pulled a stunt like that every day. Getting her way about sewing dresses for Violet didn't seem so important. Getting away from the homestead and on with her life was a lot more inviting. She took several deep breaths, then remembered how many times her own mother had gathered her up under her arm and slammed her down on a chair in the corner. One thing for sure, Emma wasn't mother material. She just plain couldn't take many more frights like that one.

Jed was whistling when he came through the door, expecting to find another nice meal and kids all happy like he'd had at the noon meal. Instead Mary was in the rocking chair facing the corner. Jimmy had his nose in his reader from school; Molly sucked her thumb. Sarah eyes darted around like she was ready to bolt out the door and run. Emma looked up from her crochet and laid it aside.

"Supper will be on the table in five minutes, Jed. By the time you wash up," she said.

"What's going on in here?" Jed didn't budge toward the dry sink.

"Mary got in trouble for walking on the well again," Jimmy said.

"You punished her?" Jed turned accusingly toward Emma.

"Yes, I did. She's been sitting in that corner for an hour and I think she is now sufficiently sorry," Emma said.

"You punished her? Just who do you think you are to deal out punishment to my kids? If she does something wrong, you wait until I come home. Is that understood?" He shook his finger under her nose like she was a child.

"We'll talk about this later." She slapped his hand away from her face. "I'll get your supper on the table now."

"We'll talk about this now," he said, an edge to his voice

that chilled her to the bone and set off a chain of sparks that resulted in pure hot anger.

"All right, then, Jed Thomas, we'll talk about it right here in front of these children, if that's what you want," she said.

"Wait a minute," Mary shoved herself out of the rocking chair. "Both of you stop it right now. Uncle Jed, don't you tell her she can't punish me. I was wrong. You told me yourself I was going to get a whoopin' if you caught me again. Jimmy told me not to do it and I did, and Emma made me sit on a chair. She was right and I was wrong. So why are you so mad at her? I'm sorry Emma. I won't never walk on the well again. I saw how it scared you and I wouldn't do that for nothing, ever again."

"You stay out of this, Mary," Jed said.

"I can't," she said. "Emma must love me like Momma did. Because that's just what Momma would have done if she would have caught me on the well. I was almighty mad at first, but after I set there a whole hour I can see I was wrong. If you say Emma can't take care of us, then who will? Are you going to come in from the plowing or fencing every time we do something we oughtn't?"

Emma bit the inside of her lip to keep from giggling. Poor Jed, caught between a rock and a hard place with no way out. "Can we please eat now before our supper gets stone cold?" she finally said. "I've got a peach cobbler in the warmer and I whipped a whole quart of fresh cream to go on the top. It's going to fall if we don't get busy."

"All right, I can see when I'm whooped," Jed said but there wasn't a bit of humor in those deep green eyes. "If Emma takes you to the wood shed next time don't you come running to me with tears in your eyes. Just remember you asked for it."

"Yes, sir." Mary smiled wanly.

Emma brushed her hair the customary one hundred strokes that night, sitting on the side of the bed with Jed behind her. Across the bolster, hands laced behind his head, staring resolutely at the rafters. She hadn't spoken a word to him during supper or since. Just laughed and talked to the children while they did their schoolwork, and taught Molly to recognize an A. In three weeks she'd probably have Molly reading from the primer on the mantel above the fireplace. In three weeks he'd be insane and would dance a jig around the front yard when she left.

"I'll take you to town tomorrow if you are ready to go," he said.

"I'm not ready," she said. "I promised three or four weeks, and I've promised to make new things for the girls. Maybe even a shirt or two for Jimmy. You can just live with it, Jed. I know you're angry with me, but I did what came natural. I wanted to shake her teeth out but that's just because she scared me so bad. So I did what my mother did when I scared her."

"Just thought I'd offer to end the deal," he said.

"Thanks but no thanks." She stretched out beside him, laced her hands behind her flowing blond hair, and stared up at the ceiling. Not a blessed thing up there to charm her like it evidently did him. "Tell me about the day of the land run, Jed. I've read all about it but you're the only person I know who ever was really there. Tell me about it."

"Why?"

"Because I want a bedtime story. Because I want to hear what it was like. Because I still can't sleep because that child frightened me so badly. What difference does it make? Forget I even asked. We can't stand each other for a few minutes, so why did I think you'd tell me a story?" She turned away from him and counted the stars around the moon.

Several minutes passed before he cleared his throat. "We rode horses and had an idea where we wanted to settle," he said finally. "It was crazy. The feeling of everyone lined up in that line. You could smell the excitement. The horses were even hard to keep in rein. Then the clear, sweet notes of a cavalry bugle rose and it seemed like it hung in the heavy excitement forever. It was straight up noon. We lashed our horses and the dust boiled up around us thicker than fog. For a while I thought I'd lost Joy. Billy and I were going to keep her between us for safety. Then she was there beside me, a gleam in her eyes like I suppose was in mine. We rode all out speed. Thank goodness we'd conditioned our horses in the weeks before or they would have dropped dead underneath us. It was like we were racing toward a goal for a little while, then the riders began to fan out and the stakes started going in the ground. We knew we wanted to be closer to Guthrie Station so we kept on riding and riding. We didn't want to be right in Guthrie so when we got close we veered off to the east, found the creek and staked our claims. We were all crying when we found the three pieces of ground together. Joy hugged me, and you should have seen her face. It was so dirty I could hardly recognize her except for her light green eyes. Billy was covered with dust and I started laughing at the two of them kissing like teenagers. They both pointed at me and it took a minute for me to realize I was as nasty as they were. We went into Guthrie and stood in line for hours to file our claim. Food was so scarce the prices were atrocious. A ham sandwich was twenty-five cents. Tents were springing up like wild mushrooms everywhere and the town went from nothing to ten thousand people in a few hours. The outlying areas weren't as congested though. By the time we got our claims filed on this land, folks were already falling out of the line and buying tickets on the next train out of Oklahoma. It wasn't what they expected, I guess. It was everything we wanted. The next week, the wagon arrived with the kids and part of the lumber. We pitched tents on the side of the creek and camped out while we built the house. A couple of more weeks later, another wagon came with the stove and Joy's sewing machine, this bed and the ones the kids use in the loft. We had the barn up by then so we lived in it until we finished the house at the end of the summer. It was against the law to sell liquor in the territory. I guess it's pretty common knowledge that the peaceful way it was settled was due to the fact that no one could get drunk. Had whiskey been available, there might have been bloodshed over the claims, but there wasn't. I can't ever tell you the feeling we had that day, though, Emma. It's not something you can describe. When I suck up a lungful of dust while I'm plowing, my heart still races thinking about the excitement of that day when the bugle sounded. We were lucky in a lot of ways. We dug a well and found good spring water. Bear Creek is the cause the neighbors got cholera and died, I'm sure. So we don't drink the water from there unless it's been boiled. I'm even scared to let the kids swim there very often in the summer. But the Cimarron is yellow and twice as bad. When we dug the well, we went through several feet of red sand after we'd cut through the sod. Then there was this gray and white sand so loose that the spade would sink in it and we almost gave up hope, then we hit real dirt and real water. Lots of men came in the rush with a wife, six kids, and forty cents in their pockets. They had grand visions of the land supporting them. We had a little money to sustain us and build a house. Oklahoma is a hard land, Emma, a land that gives up its crops grudgingly. But the whole prairie is addictive. It got in our blood and made us work twice as hard as we ever worked before. We loved it here. I still do even though it took my sister and best friend. Enough for tonight?"

"There's never enough, but I'll be satisfied. Goodnight and thank you, Jed," she said softly.

Chapter Seven

One flat iron heated on the back of the stove while Emma ironed with the other one. Molly played on the floor stringing buttons on a piece of yarn. Jed hadn't heard from his cousin, Beulah, yet. Emma dreaded the day he did. She wasn't married to Jed, not in the literal sense, but she'd gotten so attached to the children, she hated to see the day she'd have to leave them.

She'd finished five dresses the week before and true to her word, Violet had a bolt of white cotton for her on Sunday. Emma could hardly wait to get the ironing finished so she could cut out drawers and camisoles for all three girls. What she'd washed the past two Monday mornings was threadbare, barely holding together with hope and a prayer. The whole afternoon and evening she would sew for her family, and tomorrow she'd start the next job for Violet.

"My family," she snorted. It had only been two weeks since the day she had bought her ticket in Atlanta and set off to show the world she was capable of supporting herself. If she thought about herself as a governess and housekeeper for Jed's family it was easier to think of herself as succeeding. But who was she kidding? She'd gotten into a terrible mess that would follow her the rest of her life. Divorced. The word hung on the Oklahoma breeze every minute of the day. If she did fall in hopeless love someday, no respectable man would have her. Not a soiled dove. And who would believe that the dove wasn't soiled after she'd lived with a man?

"You got family?" Molly stopped playing with the buttons and looked up at Emma. "Got a little girl like Molly?"

"No, sweetheart, I don't have a little girl. I've got family in Georgia, but not a little girl," Emma said.

Molly went back to stringing buttons. She drew her eyes down as she chose the next one from the box and slipped the point of the needle into the hole. Emma wondered just what Joy had looked like. The girls all had shades of blond hair and light eyes, and she could see something of Jed in all four kids. The Thomas blood must be thicker than the Trahorn in a lot of ways. She must remember to ask Jed what his brother-in-law, Billy, looked like. She looked forward to the fifteen minutes before they actually went to sleep at night, when they talked about the past, the future, today.

The iron got cold so she replaced it with the hot one and picked one of Jed's shirts from the basket of sprinkled and rolled clothing. The maids at Crooked Oaks would be ironing Jefferson's shirts that morning. Emma wondered if her father even thought about her or if he'd simply counted his blessings when he found her note telling him she wouldn't marry Matthew, not even to keep Crooked Oaks. She'd expected him to at least send someone to find her, but then he wouldn't think to look in Guthrie. No, he'd go on to Enid and when he didn't find her there, he'd go home. He might even make Matthew his legal heir anyway. Emma shuddered just thinking about being married to that weasel for the rest of her life. Being married to Jed for three weeks and a divorcee after that wasn't as repulsive as Matthew.

A cool breeze fluttered the curtains at the kitchen window. White with rosebuds scattered on them. Emma noticed that they were stained in a few places. Maybe at the end of the week she'd have an extra wash day and do up all the curtains in the cabin. Cousin Beulah really should have a nice house to start with, and not a mess.

The distant rumble of horse hooves made her set the iron on the back of the stove and look out the front door. A buggy just like Violet's was just a dot in the distance. Emma put the teapot on a burner and picked up the iron again. "We've got company coming, Molly. Looks like Violet is bringing more fabric or else she found a minute for a cup of tea and a visit."

Molly put all the buttons back in the box, laid her string on the top and replaced the lid. She stood up, brushed the front of her calico dress and primped her hair back, just the way she'd seen Emma do before lunch time. "I'll wait for her on the porch and hold her hand."

"That will be a good job for you, Molly." Emma smiled brightly. The sound of the buggy was getting closer and closer, but Violet could drink tea and visit while Emma ironed. This wasn't Crooked Oaks with a butler, upstairs maids, gardeners, and silver trays in the foyer where people laid their cards when they came visiting. Emma was adapting, but the difference was staggering most days.

"Emma! Emma!" Molly hit the door in a run and Buster began to bark at the same time.

"Oh, no, I wasn't expecting anyone and the dog is loose." She slammed the iron down on the back burner and ran to the door. Buster wouldn't crawl right up in the buggy and bite Violet but the big old black animal would sure scare the liver right out of her with all that growling and barking.

"Buster!" she screamed as she threw the front door open and crossed the porch in three easy strides. "You come here right now," she said, putting one arm around his thick neck and grabbing for the rope hanging from the porch post with the other. Buster had always done just what she said, but he didn't right then. He shook her arm away from his neck and bounded out to the yard where the buggy had stopped. He put his front paws up on the running board and growled down deep in his throat. A menacing, protecting rumble, telling the people in the buggy that he was boss on the homestead and they weren't welcome. He'd lost his friend once before and she didn't come home for a long time. He could feel danger, and no one was taking his friend away again.

"Buster!" Emma screamed. "You come here!"

"Emma Maureen?" The driver said in a deep voice. "What is going on?"

Cold chills chased up and down her spine in waves in spite of the sweat on her brow. She shaded her eyes with the back of her hand and looked up right into the eyes of Jefferson Cummins.

Jed whistled while he plowed. He could see the house from the field and noticed that Violet had come to visit. He'd lost the battle of wills about Emma sewing those dresses but in the end, he'd won. There wasn't a woman in all of Logan County who worked as hard as Emma. She fed the family a hot breakfast, sent the children off to school, kept up the house, the washing, ironing, cooking, and scrubbing, and still had time to make dresses for Violet. The only other woman he'd ever known to work as hard was Joy—but it was her land, her kids, her home.

Things would probably slow down once Beulah arrived and Emma left, but at least he'd have some help. He might even begin to seriously look for a wife, after he got the divorce settled. His options would be limited a bit more than they had been before he married Emma. Not every man would want his daughter to be stepping out with a divorced man. But surely there was a little dark-haired, dark-eyed woman out there willing to take on four kids and make a home.

He wiped the sweat from his brow with the sleeve of his shirt. His stomach grumbled. It was still about an hour until lunch. He hoped Emma took time from the ironing to make a hot lunch. The previous week on Tuesday she had used the leftover breakfast biscuits to stuff full of thinly sliced ham and cheese, and served it up with a big bowl of hot potato soup. Sure did beat a cold biscuit and chunk of jerky in the field.

"Wonder what they talk about?" He grinned as he looked down at the house. Violet and Emma, so much alike. So independent. Was that the way women would be in the future? He'd taunted Emma about voting, but he wouldn't be a bit surprised if women did put up a squall to vote before long. At first folks would just laugh at them. After all, women weren't smart enough to know anything about politics. Crazy thought: women could run a household, settle kids' fights, sew up clothes, take care of the sick. Most likely they were smarter than menfolk when it came to voting. But he'd be laying in a six-foot hole with his hands crossed over his chest before he ever admitted such a thing to Emma.

A movement at the back of the house caught his eye. Buster coming toward him at a breakneck speed. Silly animal went everywhere that way. All four legs moving so fast they were nothing more than a blur. He shaded his eyes with the back of his hand to watch the dog and realized the movement wasn't Buster at all, but Molly. She was running one minute, stumbled and fell the next, jumped up and was running again.

"Something's wrong with Emma," he said aloud. Molly hadn't come to the fields with him since Emma arrived. He threw the reins down and started running toward Molly, his heart beating so fast he could hear the pounding in his ears.

"Jed! Jed!" she was screaming when he got close enough

to hear her screams. "Hurry, Jed. Hurry. They're taking my Emma away."

Jed swooped her up into his arms and hugged her close to his chest. "It's all right, Molly. Now, tell me what's going on?"

"Two men. They're yelling at my Emma. Buster tried to bite one of them and he said he's taking my Emma away."

"Well, let's me and you go see what we can do about that," Jed said. He carried a sobbing Molly into the kitchen through the back door. He could hear the anger in Emma's tone before he could make out the words.

"No, I will not go back to Georgia with you," Emma said coldly.

"Oh, yes, you will, and we will plan a wedding for next week," Matthew said. "Tie this dog up so I can get out of the buggy."

"I will not," Emma said. "I don't care if he tears your leg off and you bleed to death, Matthew Cross. I'm staying right here on this homestead."

"Emma Maureen, get in this buggy. This is disgraceful. You living here with this man. The sheriff said he married you, but I'll have our lawyers fix that. You can have a proper wedding with Matthew in a couple of months. Folks in Atlanta can just think you went away to visit a relative. Matthew is willing to marry you even if you are . . ." Jefferson stumbled for words.

"Even if I am what?" Emma stood her ground. She crossed her arms over her ample buxom and stared at Matthew, who leered at her.

"A soiled dove," Matthew spit out. "Marriage doesn't have to be a love match, Emma. I'll still marry you even if you have been married. What were you thinking of?" He threw his hands up in total disgust at the house, the dog and her stubbornness. Just wait until they were properly married. In six months she'd be cowering behind him like a wife should. It might take a few weeks to train her, but he was up to the task and Crooked Oaks was the incentive.

"Emma, darling, do we have guests?" Jed stepped out onto the front porch. He slipped his arm around her waist. The touch of her rigid back spoke volumes. She was angry or afraid or both.

"Yes, we do, Jed." She leaned into his embrace. The tingles playing hop-scotch up her backbone combined with the anger in her heart made for an emotional roller-coaster that she didn't know how to control. "Daddy, meet my husband, Jed Thomas. Jed, this is my father, Jefferson Cummins. And this is his friend, Matthew Cross."

"I'm her fiancé," Matthew corrected her.

Buster growled and snapped at the man's hand when he shook a finger in Emma's direction. Matthew jerked his hand back and glared at the dog.

"You were never my fiancé," Emma said.

"Would you two gentlemen like to come in for a cup of coffee, or dinner? It's about that time of day," Jed asked.

"No, we would not," Matthew said bluntly. "We've come to take Emma home. This is a foolhardy stunt she's pulled and it's over. She's going back where she belongs. I'll have my lawyer take care of this marriage thing and as soon as it is annulled, she is going to marry me. The time for her crazy hoyden ways is over. It's time someone tamed her, and I'm going to do it."

"I don't think so," Jed grinned. "Emma happens to be my wife, legal, on paper and filed at the court house. She's not going anywhere with you, Mr. Cross. She's staying here with me. This isn't a hunting dog we're fighting over; it's a woman. She's my wife so I think you'd best get on back to town and forget about taming her."

"Emma Maureen, could I talk to you in private?" Jefferson asked.

"Whatever you've got to say to me, can be said in front of my husband," she answered.

"Okay, then. Come home with me. I've been rash. I admit it. I'll have the marriage fixed. No one will ever know. You don't have to marry Matthew," he said.

"What?" Matthew sputtered.

"Hush," Jefferson whispered.

"No." Emma shook her head. "I'm not going back to Crooked Oaks. Not right now. I might come visit you later when we have time. Maybe this winter, Daddy. If I'm still welcome at the plantation. But I'm not going home with you today."

"You're my child. You'll always be welcome. It's just that you have to decide right now what's important. If you don't go home with me and Matthew today, then I won't have your marriage fixed. You'll just have to be content with being a dirt farmer's wife. Just how did you come to be married to this dirt farmer anyway?" Jefferson drew his eyebrows down in a frown.

"I've been writing to him for six months. You know how interested I was in the land run. Well, I started writing to him and he proposed. You said I had to get married in six months or else you'd leave the plantation to some charity. Of course, you meant Matthew, but I don't love him. I never did and I refuse to marry for convenience. Even if it means losing my inheritance. I came to Guthrie and we got married," she said.

"You had a ticket to Enid," Matthew snapped.

"To throw you off," she said. "And it worked. At least for a little while."

"One last time," Jefferson said. "Come home with us. Turn your back on this folly."

"No." She shook her head. "I can't."

"My Emma," Molly snubbed behind her skirt tail. "Don't go away."

"Who is that?" Matthew snarled his nose.

Molly stepped out from behind Emma. She had her thumb in her mouth and her forefinger hooked around her nose. Tears streamed down her dirty face and the hem of her dress was sagging from where she'd fallen and snagged it on green briars.

"This is Molly," Jed said. "She's the baby of my four kids."

"You married a dirt farmer with four kids already." Matthew raised his voice and Buster barked a warning.

"Yes, I did," Emma said.

Matthew's jaws worked in rage. He'd be disgraced if the people in Atlanta found out he'd been overthrown by a man with four kids. He swallowed hard and decided that Crooked Oaks was still worth the humility. If he was careful no one would even know. Like Jefferson said, they could put the word out that Emma was visiting relatives. But after the marriage he would make Emma wish she'd never been so impulsive. "Well, honey, we'll get past that, too. Call this dog off and I'll help you load your things in the boot," he said, slyly.

He didn't fool Emma one bit. The coldness in his eyes would freeze Lucifer's horns right off his head. He was willing to endure anything to get that plantation, but there was no telling how she'd have to pay for it. "My answer is no. I'm staying right here. I'll come visit later, Daddy. Maybe when there's a slow time this winter you come on back up here and we'll tell you all about our spread. Just don't bring him with you." She nodded toward Matthew. She didn't want to see him again. Not ever.

Jefferson nodded.

"You will be sorry. If this fool you've married drops dead, don't you come crawling back to me for another chance," Matthew said, setting his thin mouth in a firm, determined line. What he'd like to do was take the buggy whip and teach the big, oversized snit of a woman a lesson or two.

"If this man drops dead, I'll come looking for you, but it won't be crawling for another chance, Matthew. It will be to ask you why my husband is dead and if you had anything to do with it. Jed is a strong, healthy man. Are you making threats?" she asked.

"If that's the way you take it, then . . ." Matthew sneered.

"I think it's time for you to leave," Jed said, his eyes boring into Matthew's and seeing only a black, evil soul inside the man.

The thin hair on the top of Matthew's balding head stood straight up. He'd lost the plantation but there were other rich women in Atlanta. Women who wouldn't have to be taught how to act like a wife. "Of course it is," Matthew said. "It's evident we aren't welcome here, Jefferson. Let this foolish man have her. Maybe we'll ship her bicycle out here and her novels. Those about love in the Louisiana bayou. I'm sure she's missing both of them. And if she didn't pack her riding bloomers, she might need them too."

"Emma?" Jefferson gave her one last chance.

"Get him out of here. You're my father, and I'll always love you, but get him away from me before I sic the dog on him. Right now I'd just love to see Buster eat his leg for dinner," Emma said.

"I'll be in touch," Jefferson said. "And yes, child, you can come home for a visit any time you want."

"Thank you, Daddy. I'm sorry I disappointed you, but I not only don't love Matthew, I don't like him. Even business partners have to like each other. Have a safe trip home, and tell all the staff I miss them," she said.

Jefferson just nodded. If Jed Thomas had been a cotton planter in Georgia he might have even liked the man. He certainly seemed fond enough of Emma, standing there with his arm around her affectionately and defensively at the same time. But children? Four of them. Did that make him a grandfather? He was only forty-two years old. Not nearly old enough to be a grandfather.

"Good day, Mr. Thomas. It was nice meeting you. I wish it could have been in more pleasant circumstances." Jefferson tipped his hat toward them before he turned the horses and drove the buggy away from the yard.

"Thank you." Emma pulled away from Jed when the buggy was out of sight.

"You're quite welcome. I'll go bring the plow and horses

in now. Dinner ready at noon, or you need some more time after this?" he asked.

"It will be ready," she said. The potatoes were boiled. Potato soup, thick chunks of homemade bread, and cheese. A blackberry cobbler, made from the last jar of berries Joy had canned last summer, cooled on the back of the stove.

"Then I'll be in in about an hour." He disappeared around the house with Buster romping beside him.

"My Emma isn't going away?" Molly popped her thumb out of her mouth.

"Not right now," Emma hugged her closely. "Right now, your Emma is going to finish the last of the ironing and make us some dinner. Then we're going to make you pretty undergarments with lace and ribbons."

Molly snuggled down into Emma's shoulder and sighed.

Emma sighed with her. Her heart slowed down to a steady beat. She'd met the dragon and come away at least part victor. Her father had left the door open for her to visit but he hadn't included Jed or the children in the invitation. She didn't have to worry about that, since she was only staying two more weeks at the most. Beulah would arrive one of these days and she'd be on her way. One thing for sure, until she had word Matthew had married some other woman or dropped dead, she didn't feel safe in Georgia.

Jed sighed as he unharnessed the horses. So Emma had come from wealth, just like he'd figured the first time he laid eyes on her in that fancy get-up. She'd simply been running away from that slick golddigger sitting up there in his fancy duds beside her father. He looked rich enough in his own right, but from the drift of the argument he had his eyes set on her father's plantation, as well. He wondered if Emma would have come to her senses and gone back to marry Matthew Cross if Jed hadn't gotten dragged into the picture and married her. If he'd lost a woman like Emma, who could do anything in the world, and a big cotton plantation to boot, he might be shooting daggers, too.

"A bicycle and love novels," he muttered, hanging the

harness up on the right nails and rubbing a little saddle soap into them. "So what? Joy loved to ride her bicycle when we lived in Nebraska. Billy and I rode our bicycles with her. We would have brought them down here with us if it would have been feasible. Can't hardly ride a bicycle in this part of the territory. Up one hill, down another and fighting scrub oak, post oak, and black jack trees as well as green briars all the way. Joy liked love stories, too. She and Emma would have gotten along real good, I'm thinking."

It didn't matter that his sister was independent and gone from the face of this earth. Nor did it matter that Emma had some of the same ideas. Emma would be gone as soon as Beulah arrived. Jed almost wished he hadn't been so quick in sending that letter to Beulah. But what was done, was done and couldn't be undone. Maybe Beulah wouldn't want to leave Texas. Jed shook his head physically to get rid of that notion. The quicker Emma was out of his life, the faster things could have some semblance of normalcy. Nothing would ever make sense as long as that tall blond was around.

Chapter Eight

The church was packed in spite of the low-hanging dark clouds on the horizon. Emma sat beside Jed, closer than she ever was to him at home, except for the day when her father and Matthew appeared. He'd done a good job of putting on a show of normalcy in front of them, but after that he didn't touch her at all. The kids kept them busy and apart during the day. That and their own determination and the bolster did its job at night.

"Let us begin this morning's services by singing 'The Old Rugged Cross'," Preacher Elgin announced in a booming voice.

By the time Jed found the hymn in the book, the first verse was finished and the whole church was into the second one from sheer memory. When the last words of the hymn had been sung, the preacher went right into a sermon from Matthew 5 concerning all the blessings people could

91

obtain if they worked those qualities mentioned in that chapter into their lives.

Emma listened with one ear and wondered if Anna Marie was listening at all. She was sitting so close to some fellow that Emma figured they might have to get a surgeon to separate them after the services. Evidently she'd brought Alford to Sunday morning services to show Jed as well as the rest of the congregation that she was pretty enough to get any man. It didn't have to be Jed Thomas, with his quiet manner, tall good looks, and downright sexy smile.

Alford had red hair, a haphazard attempt at a mustache, and light blue eyes. He was only a few inches taller than Anna Marie and for some odd reason reminded Emma of Matthew. Must be the banker's attitude. Matthew was the vice-president of the bank where Jefferson did his business in Atlanta, and Alford's mannerisms were so close to Matthew's that Emma couldn't help but think they must have attended the same school.

"Now, for the social announcements," Preacher Elgin said.

Emma shook the cobwebs from her head, realizing that she'd been letting her mind wander rather than listening to the sermon. Molly popped her thumb out of her mouth and got ready to run outside to play with her little friends for a few minutes before they all loaded up in their wagons and went back home. Jimmy fidgeted in the pew. Sarah and Mary squirmed. It had been a long hour.

"My daughter Anna Marie would like to announce her engagement and upcoming marriage to Alford Manor. They are planning a wedding in two weeks. She tells me it will take place on Sunday, right after morning services, and there will be a pot-luck reception on the church grounds. So all you ladies are to be thinking about your favorite recipes and frocks," Preacher Elgin smiled. "And now church is dismissed. You young'uns have been still long enough," he said.

There were a few giggles and a rush of warm, humid air

as the back door opened and the youth fled the rigid seats and quietness. Emma followed Jed to the end of the pew to the center aisle. Anna Marie and Alford, Jed and Emma were the last four in the church by that time. Anna Marie held Alford's arm, pressing her ribs into it so tightly that Emma reinforced her idea that they were permanently united. Perhaps the lady had learned a valuable lesson. Never let the man out of her sight or he might bring home a wife to introduce to her.

"Well, Jed Thomas, how are you today? Please meet my fiancé, Alford Manor. We'll sure expect to see you at our wedding next month." Anna Marie smiled brightly, and rudely ignored Emma.

"It's a pleasure." Jed shook hands with Alford.

"And you must be Mrs. Thomas." Alford extended his hand toward Emma. His handshake was firm but his eyes were cold when he looked up at her. One more quality just like Matthew. "I understand you used to live in Atlanta, Georgia. Your father came by the bank, asking questions the other day. I sent him to the sheriff. I trust he found you?"

"Of course," Emma smiled. "The sheriff gave him wonderful directions out to our homestead. We had a really nice visit. He plans to come again in the winter perhaps when the cotton crop isn't demanding every moment of his time. Thank you for assisting him."

Alford wrinkled his brow. That wasn't at all the answer he expected from Emma. He'd heard through the hot little Guthrie gossip grapevine that Emma had run away from a wealthy family and her father had come to take her back home. Until that moment he had pictured her as a weak, plain-looking girl without a brain in her head. She was none of those things. She towered above him, shook hands as firm as a man, and looked like she could boss a logging crew.

"You are quite welcome. Anna Marie and I will see you

at our wedding?" He posed the question and felt Anna Marie tense at the same time.

Emma tried to think of a way to say yes, she would be there without actually lying. By the day of the wedding, she'd be long gone. Beulah would be there for sure by then, but Emma did not want Anna Marie to know she was leaving. Not after she'd said such hateful things at the church picnic. Ugly. That's the word she'd said. Big and ugly.

"Emma, hurry, hurry, it's starting to rain. We've got to hurry home." Sarah ran up to Emma's side. "Uncle Jed, let's go," she said, tugging on his hand.

Thank you, Lord, for a few raindrops and a child, she prayed silently as they ran to the wagon where the children were already loaded in the back. Jed seated her, then picked up the reins and hurried the horses on the way to the homestead two miles back to the west. By the time they got home, rain had started in earnest and all six of them were soaked to the skin. Jed stopped at the house long enough to let Emma and the children out, then drove to the barn to unhitch the wagon and put the horses in stables.

The weight of the water caused her hair to come undone from its tidy bun and string down her back and over her shoulders. Even her drawers and corset were drenched. Emma had never felt more like a big, ugly giant in her life as she stepped into the living room of the cabin. "Okay, children, take your shoes off and line them up right here beside the wall. They'll dry by tomorrow morning. Then skinny yourselves up the ladder and come out of every stitch of clothing you have on. Toss them over the railing and I'll put them in a pile for tomorrow's laundry. We surely don't want any of you to get sick."

"My new underwear is all soaked. Will it mess up my ribbons?" Molly sobbed.

"No, they'll be just fine," Emma assured her. "I'm going in the bedroom to find dry clothing. When I get done we'll make some dinner."

Lightning streaked through the sky and thunder rolled as

Jed trotted from the barn to the house. He was already wet to the skin but the rain seemed colder. Like the south wind might bring in a hailstorm with it. He hoped not. Alfalfa was just pushing up out of the plowed fields, not to mention vegetable garden or the acres of cotton he'd planted. Hail would take them right back to square one. The garden would have to be replanted and the root cellar was getting emptier by the day.

"Yuk," he muttered as he slung the back door open and stopped just inside the door to take his boots off. He could wring water from his Sunday trousers, and the starch Emma put in his white shirt was making the wet thing stick to his skin like it had been washed in pure honey.

"How come water feels so good on Saturday night for a bath, or when we go to the creek to swim, and so awful when the rain soaks us?" Jimmy asked as he climbed back down the ladder. He wore a soft, clean shirt and had combed his brown hair back just like Jed wore his. His pants were ironed with a crease in the legs. Straight as a judge passing judgment, as Joy would say if she could see them.

"Don't make a lick of sense to me, Jimmy," Jed said.

"Well, what are you waitin' for? Go in there and shuck out of them clothes and get some dry ones on." Jimmy pointed to the bedroom.

The door was closed, so Emma must be in there doing just what Jimmy told him to do. The bolster might divide the bed but it sure couldn't take care of this problem. "I'll just wait for Emma," Jed mumbled.

"Why? Daddy and Momma went to the bedroom to-gether to get dressed. They was married. That's what mar-ried folks do, Uncle Jed," Jimmy whispered.

"Well, I see you got even wetter." Emma saved the day by opening the door. "You better get on in there and change before you catch your death of pneumonia, Jed Thomas. The venison should be ready by now. I'll just have to steam some rice and open up some green beans."

She'd brushed her hair back and tied it with a ribbon. Her face was shiny clean and Jed thought she was absolutely beautiful in the faded calico dress.

"Whatever are you two staring at? Do I have my dress buttoned crooked?" She looked down to make sure she hadn't done just that in her haste to get out of the room and let Jed have a turn.

"Nothing," Jimmy said. "Just that you look so different with your hair down and in that dress."

"It's my work frock. I usually just used it to do garden work." She didn't mention it was the first thing she came to in her trunk and she knew Jed would be needing to get out of wet clothes promptly. "Get on, Jed. I'll start the rice."

He just nodded. If only she wasn't so tall and so bossy. She had a nice way with the children and her cooking was something to die for. He shut the door and peeled the wet clothes from his body. Just how did she learn so much in that rich house anyway? They must have a whole staff of servants living on a plantation like that, and yet there didn't seem to be one thing she couldn't do.

Emma used the tail of her apron to open the stove door. The aroma of fresh roast venison wafted through the cabin and Jimmy padded barefoot to her side to sniff even deeper of the aroma. She grabbed for real hotpad holders and pulled the cast-iron dutch oven out, set it on top of the stove, and lifted the heavy lid. It was done to perfection, the juices ready to make into a rich, dark gravy. She took a loaf of bread down from a shelf above the dry sink and sliced it while Jimmy watched.

Jed's heart must be broken in half. There he was, all ready to marry Anna Marie before she stepped into the picture. Now Anna Marie was engaged to another man just to get back at Jed. It was all a mess. Emma wasn't really married to Jed, who wanted to be married to Anna Marie, who was really going to marry Alford when she was in love with Jed. It would take forever to untangle the whole sordid affair and no one would ever believe that she and Jed were never married except on paper.

She wiped a tear away from her heavy eyelash. She should have just spoken up and told Alford that she wouldn't be at the wedding because she was leaving as soon as Beulah arrived. That way if Anna Marie wanted to wait for Jed to get divorced, she could. Just because she didn't like the girl, certainly didn't mean that Jed wasn't madly in love with her. She promised herself that she would be honest with Anna Marie the very next time she saw her. It wouldn't be until the next Sunday but she would walk right up to her and tell her the truth. That she was leaving Logan County and Jed would be getting a divorce so if Anna Marie wanted to wait for that she could have him.

"What's the matter?" Jimmy asked seriously.

"Nothing," Emma said.

"Then why did you nearly cry?"

"I didn't. Steam got in my eyes," she said. "Now, why would I cry? We've got rain coming down in buckets just like Jed said we needed. Sunday dinner will be ready soon as the rice is steamed. Maybe I'll make a pudding out of what is left over for tomorrow night. Open that jar of beans. We better get them in the pan so they can boil fifteen minutes while the biscuits cook." She talked to cover up the truth that Jimmy had seen in her eyes. So what if she was developing some kind of crazy feelings for her legal husband? He sure didn't give a care about her. She wasn't his type. To be truthful, she wasn't any man's type. She was too tall, too big, too independent. All men liked little bitty swooning women who were willing to trail along in their dust. Women who didn't have two healthy brain cells to rub together. Who could never think enough to form an opinion about anything.

"Smells good out here," Jed said, shoving open the bedroom door. "Here Jimmy, let me help you." He took the jar from the boy and twisted the lid off on the first try.

"Why do you boil them fifteen minutes?" Jimmy asked, watching Emma add slivers of onion and a heaping tablespoon of bacon drippings out of the skillet where she'd fried bacon for breakfast.

"To keep you from getting sick," she said. "Sarah, you and Mary hurry up and get down here to set the table."

"Yes, ma'am." The voices blended as one and floated down from the loft.

The storm got worse as they ate dinner. Jed finally lit the kerosene lamp they kept in the middle of the table. The sky turned a strange shade of green and the rain stopped. The silence was even more eerie than the darkness in the middle of the day. A cold breeze stole through the open front door and made the girls squeal that their bare feet were freezing.

"Ah, you're just a bunch of cream puffs," Jed said.

"What's a cream puff, really, Emma?" Jimmy asked.

"It's a wonderful dessert. A puffy pastry filled with whipped cream and sprinkled with sugar. I'll make them for you one day soon," she said, handing the platter of venison down the table to Jed.

"Mighty fine vittles," he mumbled. It was amazing what Emma had done with the deer he'd shot on Thursday. She'd helped him butcher the meat, canned several jars of it, made jerky out of one haunch, and hung one in the spring house to keep it cool enough until Sunday dinner. Thursday night she'd fried steaks for supper. Friday night they had a stew made from meat she'd cut into one-inch cubes and cooked slowly with carrots, potatoes, and onions. Saturday, they'd had the last of the pork chops from the smoke house just to give them a break from venison. Then today there was a wonderful roast. If Emma hadn't been there at least half of the meat would have gone to waste.

To top it all off, she'd fussed about the hide so he'd stretched it out, scraped the underside until it was clean, and was drying it with the hair intact for an area rug. She declared it would be wonderful in the wintertime to keep the children from having to sit on the cold wood floor.

"It's kind of strange out there." Emma hugged herself against the odd feeling inside. "Almost green cast, isn't it? And that odd noise off in the distance. It sounds like the train I rode on, Jed. Yet, I know the station is too far away for us to ever hear the trains."

"I don't hear anything," Jed said, looking up from his plate.

"I do," Molly said. "Like the day those mean men came to take my Emma away. Only it's not a train track. It's a bunch of horses pulling a big wagon. Way far off. If you listen real close you can hear it."

"No," Jed whispered. He'd heard about the tornadoes but never experienced one. The signs were all there, just like John Whitebear told him about. A strange aura like the sky was seeping a green mist. Cold wind on his feet but not his face. A south wind and a noise like thundering buffalo in the distance. Or a train.

"What?" Emma caught the fear in his voice.

"Okay, we're going to the root cellar right now," Jed stood up. "I'll carry Molly. Everyone hold hands and don't let go."

"But why?" Emma asked.

"Just take my hand," he said, holding his free hand toward her. "I think it might be a tornado we're feeling. If it is we'll be safe in the root cellar."

Sarah whimpered but one look from Emma and she sucked it right up. Mary rolled her eyes but she gave Jimmy her hand and they all proceeded out of the house like a human rope. The noise was deafening by the time they were across the lawn and the funnel cloud was approaching fast out of the southwest.

"Look Emma, at that funny black thing. It's swirling around," Molly pointed.

"I know, baby. Let's get you kids down in the cellar right now. Jimmy, when I was down there getting potatoes I saw a match beside the lantern. You go first and get it lit," she said, squeezing Jed's hand as if he were her lifeline.

Jed handed Molly to Emma and slammed the big, heavy wooden door shut when he started down the rickety stairs into the dugout which was little more than a cave. If his whole farm wasn't wiped out by the tornado, the first thing he intended to do was do some work on the cellar. It wasn't fit for the children or Emma either. If he ever had to get his chubby cousin, Beulah, down the stairs, he'd be in big trouble.

A dim light shined from the back of the cellar when Jimmy got the coal oil lantern lit. Joy had been adamant in having a cellar so she could keep her potatoes, carrots, onions, and beets all year. Not to mention the three bushel baskets of pecans stacked in the corner. He and Billy had fussed and fumed about the job but right then he was glad they had dug it and made the wooden steps and door. If that storm did the kind of damage the Indians told him about, they might have to live in the root cellar until he could rebuild.

A fierce wind tore at the door. Emma stared at the chain Jed had hooked around a ten-penny nail that had been driven into the framework of the stairs. Sarah covered her ears with her hands and Molly tried to melt herself into Emma's shoulder. Emma wanted to do the same thing— only in Jed's shoulder. What she wouldn't give to be a whimpering woman right at that moment couldn't be measured in money. Just to be able to cuddle up in his arms and know the safety of real love.

"How long does it last?" she finally asked.

"I don't know," Jed said seriously, shaking his head. "The Indians told me about tornadoes. Said there would be a silence after the rain. That weird, strange color in the sky and then the noise of a herd of buffalo. I just hope it leaves something standing up there. It can pick up a house and take it miles away to throw it back down on the ground with enough force to smash it to smithereens."

"Is it going to take my new drawers with the lace and ribbons?" Molly asked, mortified. "Uncle Jed, go up there and tell it to go away."

"I wish I could baby. I surely wish I could," he said.

It seemed like hours and hours of the deafening noise. But when Jed checked his pocket watch only twenty minutes had elapsed from the time they slammed the door shut until there was nothing but the patter of soft rain outside. He unhooked the chain and hefted the door open with his shoulder, saying a prayer as he did. *Please, God, don't let my house be destroyed.*

"It's still there," he said, breathing a sigh of relief.

Emma followed him out of the cellar and the barefoot kids trailed along behind her. She would have taken all of them to Georgia on the next train if the homestead had been wiped out. They were, after all, the equivalent of her children, and Jefferson Cummins could have just dealt with it. But the house was still standing. She could see holes in the barn roof, and a board was protruding out of the kitchen window like the sword in that story she read once. Strange that should come to her mind. A sword stuck in a stone and only someone with a pure heart could remove it.

"Oh, no," Mary said dramatically. "It's broke the window and look at the floor. The wind blew the door open and it's all wet with rain. And Emma, look at the table. That chunk of wood broke your plate."

It's an omen. I should have never been here, she thought as she picked up a rag mop from the corner and commenced to sopping up an inch of water covering most of the floor. "There are other plates. You girls all get on back upstairs and change out of those wet things again. I'll surely have a big wash day tomorrow. Jed, you better check on the barn and see how much damage we've got there before you change again. Jimmy, you can go with him."

"You sure you're all right?" Jed asked.

"I'm fine. We'll have this put to rights by the time you get back. If you'd bring a board or two for the window.

You'll have to shut it up. I'll miss it but we can't have the weather and mosquitoes coming inside," she said. But Emma's insides were opposite from fine. They were a quivering mess.

"Buster!" Molly screamed from the loft after Jimmy and Jed had took off out the back door toward the barn. "Where is my Buster?"

"Oh, no." Emma remembered the dog had scampered under the front porch when they all ran to the cellar. She hadn't seen him since. "You get dry, Molly. Sarah, help her. I'll check on Buster."

She lifted her sopping wet shirttail and went outside. A soft summer rain fell so gently it was hard to think that just minutes ago a vicious storm had torn through the countryside. "Buster, where are you?" she yelled, but he didn't bound around the edge of the porch like he usually did. She gathered her skirts even higher and peeped under the porch. No Buster.

She started around the house. Perhaps he'd taken refuge in the barn with the horses and would be running from that direction. She called again. Still no Buster. Then she saw him, laying on his side right under the kitchen window. The same length of rough wood that broke the window and her plate evidently had hit him first, because the end rested right beside his head. Blood trickled out of the wound and his eyes were shut.

She dropped down on her knees in the mud and laid her head on his chest, tears flowing down her cheeks. There was a steady heartbeat, so she knew that he wasn't dead. She picked him up gently and waded through the mud back around the house. "Open the door, Sarah," she called out. "Buster's been hurt."

A flurry of action filled the house as she took Buster to the bedroom and laid him on the rug beside the bed. Three little girls and a grown woman grabbed towels to dry one big, black dog's fur and clean his head wound. By the time he opened his eyes and whimpered pitifully, they were all crying. When he stood up and shook his wet fur, they giggled nervously and tried to hug him all at the same time.

"What's going on?" Jimmy asked from the door. "Uncle Jed is going to be mad if he finds that dog in the house."

"That's right," Jed said right behind him. "You all know the rules. No pets inside the house."

"Well, you can just get mad," Emma bowed up to him. "Buster is hurt. His head is bleeding. I carried him in here because I thought he was dying, and he's my friend, so he's staying right there until he feels better."

"Let me see," Jed said, bending down to take a closer look.

"The wood that broke the window felled him," Emma said.

"Then I expect he'd better stay in until he's a little better," Jed said, biting his lip to keep from grinning. "But he's not sleeping on my bed, and that's an order."

"All of you get out of here. I need to change clothes. Again." Emma moaned at the muddy mess her dress was in.

Jimmy stopped in the middle of the bedroom floor. "But why does Uncle Jed have to get out? You two are married, aren't you?"

Jed grinned and rolled his eyes. Emma blushed scarlet.

"We're going to clean up the rest of the water, and you can help, Jimmy. Just because you are a boy don't mean you can't do some things in the house." Sarah got him by the shirt sleeve. "Soon as you get out of those muddy clothes, you can squeeze the mop for us."

Mary slammed the door, leaving Jed, Emma, and Buster in the room together. "That's right, Jimmy. Change your clothes and then come help us girls." Mary issued the order just like Sarah had done. Wait until tomorrow morning. She could hold court about how romantic the whole storm had been and how Jed and Emma had looked at each other so sweetly when it was over. Just like a love story in a book that her friend Hannah's mother read all the time. Hannah even sneaked around and read one of them when her momma was gone to the store and she got to be queen when she told all the girls about the story. When Mary got big enough she might even write love stories. It would shock the whole world but she could already envision her name on the back of a big thick book.

"Now what?" Emma asked.

"Now you get your things and go to your side of the bed with your big black friend and I'll take mine to my side of the bed. We'll turn our backs, trust each other and not turn around until we both are dressed. It's all we can do," Jed said.

"I suppose so," she agreed, but her knees were like jelly when she slipped out of her camisole. Surely after all the nights of sleeping with Jed she could trust him to keep his word and not sneak peeks at her naked backside. *He's always been a gentleman,* she reminded herself.

And always will be, her conscience said. *A gentleman who isn't interested in you.*

Chapter Nine

The sun was high and unusually hot for the end of May. Jed lazed back on the quilt, listened to the children squealing, and hoped Oklahoma wasn't in for a drought. They'd wanted to swim in the creek but he still worried about cholera. Besides, they would have had to slide down a red clay embankment to even get to the water. So he'd vetoed that idea real quick and Emma didn't even argue. Evidently she realized she'd never get all that red stain out of their clothing. The natural farm pond was at waist deep on Sarah and the water was clean. At least for now, it was. If they didn't get rain soon the water would stagnate and the children wouldn't swim anymore this summer. He wouldn't take the chance, not after losing Joy and Billy both to the disease last winter.

He shut his eyes and folded his hands across his chest. Life was good right then. School had ended for the year. The preacher's wife, Myrtle, had agreed to teach the next year if they couldn't find anyone else to take the job. The children were excited at the prospect of three months of freedom. By the end of summer they'd all be whining to get back into the routine. Mary might wither up and drop graveyard dead without daily contact with her friends. Sarah and Jimmy would be happy with Sunday visits and picnics on the church lawn occasionally. He still hadn't heard from Beulah, but that didn't mean anything. She might send a telegram or a letter, or she might show up on his doorstep one day. Until that time, things were going just fine.

Emma leaned against a pecan tree and watched the children and dog playing in the water. The whole picnic had been her idea and Jed had even agreed without a fight, which was a miracle within itself. Most days the two of them couldn't agree on anything. The dog shouldn't be in the house, not even lying at her feet while she sewed. She was too tough on the kids. She wasn't tough enough on the kids. He'd fuss about one meal that she slaved over for hours and compliment her cooking another time when all she did was throw something together.

She figured he'd refuse to even consider taking a whole day from work just to play. But he had agreed that they could have a picnic from sunup to sundown. A day of play just to celebrate the finish of another year of school. Swimming and eating. Napping under the shade tree if anyone got tired. Ball games in the afternoon. Three on one team. Three on the other. They even had a bat and ball he'd found amongst his things in the barn.

The girls looked cute in their bathing costumes she'd designed for them as a surprise. Emma smiled when she remembered Molly's questions about what kind of dresses she was making that looked like that. Sarah wore a bathing dress made from a blue striped feedsack. Mary's was pink checks and Molly's was pure white, left over from the cotton lawn she'd made their undergarments from. No sleeves, a scoop neckline, buttons down the back, a big sash on top

of pantaloon bottoms cuffed just below the knee. Such freedom to romp and play in the water without a long wet
dresstail tangled up around their feet. Emma wished she
had the courage to put on a bathing costume and play with
them.

Jimmy had shucked his shirt and rolled up an old pair
of trousers and the three older kids were attempting to swim
in the shallow water. If only they were back at Crooked
Oaks with the bubbling, clear creek water she'd learned to
swim in. If only! Two words that haunted her every day.
They made more splash than anything but Emma enjoyed
watching them. She dreaded the day she'd have to tell them
all good-bye. Four little kids who'd stolen her heart away.

"What are you thinking about? Getting back to that plantation without all the work?" Jed asked, cocking one eye
open.

"Momma said staying busy made a happy woman," she
said softly.

"Why didn't your mother come with your father to find
you?" he asked.

"Momma died when I was sixteen. She went to work in
her rose garden and we found her there. A beautiful day
just like this one. She'd only been gone for a little while.
She was still warm." Emma's voice came from far away,
somewhere deep in her soul.

"I'm sorry," Jed said.

"Thank you. Momma was my best friend. She taught me
to ride the bicycle and to read novels. Daddy didn't like
my independence. Still doesn't. He thought he could tame
me by making me marry Matthew. I don't like Matthew.
He's got a mean streak in him that Daddy can't see and
wouldn't believe me if I told him. I've seen him kick horses
and dogs. To answer your question, no, I wasn't missing
the plantation," she said.

"Then you aren't regretting not marrying Matthew?" Jed
asked.

"Not one bit. I told you I'm not the marrying kind of

woman. I like being independent. I might go to the capital someday and lead a march to the White House lawn for women to vote. I might write love stories or ride in a bicycle race. Men don't like women like me, Jed."

"I see," he said. But he didn't see at all. Why would Emma work so hard at making a home if she didn't want one of her own? What she said contradicted itself. She'd planned the day for the children. She sewed for Violet and used the money to buy fabric to make Sarah, Mary, and Molly extra things. She cooked. She ironed. She mended and cleaned. She loved Molly like a mother. Yet, she claimed she wasn't mother and wife material. None of it made a bit of sense to Jed.

"Uncle Jed, come in with us and throw us over your shoulder," Mary pleaded.

"No. I'm going to lay right here and let the sun soak into these tired old bones," he said.

"Please, please, please," Sarah begged.

He opened both eyes and grinned at Emma. A boyish grin that deepened the slight cleft in his chin and the single dimple in the left side of his cheek. A grin that could have made her gasp for air and fall fanny over tea kettle in love if he'd been a southern dandy in Georgia.

"Suppose I could play for a little while. I did tuck in an old pair of pants with holes in the knees just in case," he said. "Maybe I'll throw Emma in the water." He raised an eyebrow rakishly.

"I didn't bring extra clothes. And darlin' Jed, you'd better go home and get your dinner if you intend to throw me in the water, because it'll be an all-day job, honey." She smiled, her eyes twinkling.

"Don't challenge me, Emma." His green eyes glittered and the cleft in his chin deepened with the grin.

"Don't threaten me, Jed," she retorted.

"You should have made yourself one of those bathing things," Jed said.

"You mean you would let your wife wear one of those?" she asked.

"Of course. You'd look lovely in one with those nice long legs," he said, flirting with his wife and enjoying every minute of it.

"Thank you, I think," she said, blushing.

In a few minutes he dropped his shirt, pants and the rest of his clothing into the back of the wagon. He tip-toed barefoot and gingerly to the edge of the pond where all the children immediately began to splash water on him. "Hey, hey, let me ease into this. Holy smoke, you urchins didn't tell me the water was this cold. You're all going to be sick."

"It's only cold at first," Jimmy said.

Emma realized Jed Thomas was handsome, but seeing him wearing only a pair of faded, worn pants and no shirt just about took her breath away. He'd always slept in his long underwear, buttoned all the way up to his neck, sleeves down to his wrists, and pantlegs all the way to his ankles. He'd rolled the legs of the trousers up to his knees and soft dark hair covered his legs as well as his chest. She'd love to touch his chest just one time to see if it was indeed as soft as it looked. Did all men have hair on their bodies like that? she wondered. Or just men with dark hair like Jed? She couldn't imagine balding Matthew having muscles all covered with hair. Or Alford Manor either. Had Anna Marie been swimming with them before? If she had it was no wonder she was so angry at Emma for stealing her man.

"My Emma," Molly called. "Come and put your feet in the water like Momma."

"Joy used to sit on the bank and cool her feet," Jed called out to her. "Molly won't get you wet like these hooligans." Jed tossed Jimmy over his head and out into the center of the pond.

"Okay, Molly, it does look tempting," Emma said. She unlaced her shoes and pulled her stockings down from mid-thigh. She rolled up the legs of her lace-bottomed drawers until they were at her kneecaps, heisted her petticoat and dress tail, and tip-toed to the edge of the water.

"Tenderfoot!" Jed called out. He was grinning like a schoolboy. Like he did the first time he and a bunch of boys hid in the bushes and watched several girls swim in their undergarments. He hoped she thought he was just enjoying the water and not the sight of her legs. Such long shapely legs that made his mouth dry.

"You walked like a duck so don't call me a tenderfoot," she snipped. She sat down on the grassy bank and dangled her feet in the cold water. It surely did feel wonderful. She could absolutely weep for not making herself a swimming outfit so she could duck her whole body into the water. So he thought she had nice long legs, did he?

"Oh, that's wonderful," she murmured.

"Momma liked it, too," Molly said. "Look at my rocks." She pointed to a stack of smooth, small rocks she'd collected and stacked at the edge of the water.

"Oh, Molly, they're very pretty. What are you going to do with them?" Emma reached forward and touched the top one.

"Take them home and make a flower bed," Molly said seriously. "My Emma will help me."

"Of course I will. We'll use them to outline a flower bed right beside the garden. Jed can see if he can get us some marigold seeds when he goes to the general store in a few weeks. They'll bloom this fall and come up again next year."

"Okay," Molly said, fishing around in the bottom of the shallow water for more rocks. "I hear another storm. Horses coming." She cocked her head off to one side and listened.

Emma checked the southwest. No clouds. Not even a single little white puff. Just endless summer blue sky and hot sunshine, but she could hear the same noise. Only it sounded like it was coming from the east. Then she could see the dust boiling and several horsemen riding right toward them.

"John!" Molly squealed. "Indian John." She was out of the water and running toward the horses before Emma could stop her.

"Jed!" Emma screamed. "The horses will run over her. Help!"

"No, they won't," Jed said, climbing up the grassy bank so close to Emma she could smell the coolness of him. "I'll get my shirt right quick. Watch John. He's going to grab her right off the ground. He's done it for a year. She loves him."

Sure enough, John Whitebear rode like wildfire until he was right beside the child. He reached down with one arm, swooped her up, and the horses never missed a single beat. Emma stood up, shaking her petticoat and dress tail down over her bare feet. When the Indians were only a few feet away, they reined them in, and the ponies stopped so quickly it took her breath away.

"Mrs. Thomas, you have a runaway papoose. I have brought her home to you," John Whitebear grinned, handing Molly down.

Jed slipped his shirt on but didn't button it. "I thought you might be riding with your wife and daughters this time." He shook hands with John and nodded toward the other Indians with him.

"So that's the reason you try to cover all that fur on your chest," John laughed. "My daughters and wife would think that was very funny. We are out hunting deer today. Seen any tracks?"

"Shot a big one last week about a mile north of here. Looked like a small herd. Might still be there. Want to join us for the noon meal? We've brought enough food for an army," Jed said.

"No, we'll go on," John said. "I can't believe you are playing, Jed Thomas. I've told you for a long time to use a little time for resting. Your new wife is good for you. Maybe I will bring my wife and daughters to meet her soon."

"That would be good," Jed said, wondering just how long Emma would be there. If John Whitebear wanted his family to meet her, he'd better not play around too long. "Good luck on the hunt. If you don't find the herd, come by the house on your way back and we'll share some jars of canned meat with you. Emma put up several jars from the buck I killed."

"Thank you Jed Thomas." John was on his pony and gone without another word, just a wave and a smile to Molly.

"More storm," Molly said, pointing toward the west this time.

Emma shaded her eyes with the back of her hand. One lone rider, didn't seem to be in a hurry, and most definitely was a female riding sidesaddle. An uneasy feeling seized Emma's heart and squeezed tightly. It was supposed to be their day. A relaxing time of fun for the kids as well as for her and Jed. She didn't really mind sharing it with the Indians for a few moments. But something told her she wasn't going to like sharing it with whomever was invading their privacy this time.

She tried to shake off the heavy feeling but it wouldn't go away. Especially when the rider was close enough that she could see Anna Marie's dark hair and Sunday best frock. She bit her lip to keep back the moan of disgust. She'd promised herself she'd be honest with the girl the very next time she saw her, and that was the very last thing she wanted to do. Emma noticed that Jed had hurriedly buttoned his shirt and was busy rolling his pants legs down. Seeing his grin and mossy green eyes watching Anna Marie dismount made Emma want to slap both of them.

"Well, hello." Anna Marie smiled brightly at Jed and ignored Emma, just like she always did. "I was in Guthrie looking at wedding dress material. Alford and I looked at a small house he is going to buy for us to live in. A cute little place right in town. The man who runs the telegraph office owns it. When I told him where I lived, he said he was on his way to Dodsworth with a telegram for you and I offered to bring it along since I was on my way back home. I didn't think about finding you all out here. Saves me a mile of riding. Help me down, Jed?" She reached for him and he had to either catch her or she would have fallen on the ground.

"Thank you," he said, reaching out for the piece of paper and shoving it into his pile of dry clothing. "I appreciate you bringing it."

"Aren't you going to read it?" she asked.

"Not right now," he said.

The children were still splashing in the water. Emma towered above Anna Marie and felt like a fifth wheel on a wagon right then. The tableau was something right out of one of Kate's bayou love stories. The beautiful jilted lady in her Sunday best. The plain wife in her faded work dress. The rogue of a man, looking so handsome that both women wanted him.

The silence as well as the idea of wanting Jed suffocated Emma. She should ask Anna Marie for a private word but she wasn't about to tell the witch one thing when she ignored her very presence.

"Well, I'll be on my way, Jed," Anna Marie said. "Did I tell you Alford has ordered me a beautiful wedding ring with diamonds in it? He says the best is barely good enough for me."

"I'm glad you are so much in love," Jed said.

"Love?" Anna Marie said, giggling. "Darlin' I don't love Alford. I'm marrying him because he'll make a good husband. I'll always love you."

Emma had to jerk her lower lip up and bite down on it to keep it from sagging all the way to her knees. The woman had no dignity at all. If Emma had really been a wife to Jed, she would have yanked all that black hair out and enjoyed every moment of doing it. It was evident that Jed didn't know what to say. Emma almost felt sorry for him. He was in a loveless marriage and more than likely, he'd always be in love with Anna Marie.

"Well, I'll be on my way, darlin'," Anna Marie said. "Don't forget Sally is getting married tomorrow. I'm standing up with her and we'll have a dinner on the grounds afterwards. We'll all look forward to seeing you and the children. Good-bye, Jed."

"Good-bye," he said, helping her back into the saddle.

She'd barely turned the horse around when Buster finally noticed the wicked woman he hated so bad was right next to his friend. He bounded out of the water and hit the bank with the hair on his back standing straight up as he growled a warning to the dark-haired human to leave his friend alone.

"Buster!" Jed hollered but the dog kept coming as fast as his four sturdy legs would carry him.

"Buster!" Emma tried to stop him but he ignored her, too.

"You keep that mangy mutt away from me," Anna Marie screamed at the same time he snapped at her feet.

The dog's snapping jaws spooked the horse, who took off like a coyote after a jack rabbit. Emma watched in a trance as the horse galloped, Anna Marie struggled to hang on and Buster tried to bite her feet, and Jed chased behind the whole bunch of them yelling at Buster to heel. Finally the dog gave up the race and ran back to Jed. He'd gotten rid of the wicked human and would go back to his family. Jed panted, completely out of breath, and watched Anna Marie finally fall from the horse's back and land like a rag doll in the green grass.

Emma sucked in a lungful of air and held it. Anna Marie just laid there. She didn't get up or move. Before Emma even realized what she was doing she was running barefoot through the tall grass to help the girl. Jed beat her by only a few steps and was holding Anna Marie in his arms when Emma arrived. Anna Marie opened her eyes slyly and winked at Emma, then fluttered her lashes and moaned, laying her cheek on Jed's chest. "Oh, Jed, darlin', I'm hurt," she whispered. "How am I ever going to get home?"

"I'll drive you home in the wagon." He stood up, keeping her tightly in his arms. "Emma, you stay here and watch the children. I'll only be gone an hour."

"You won't leave me until I'm okay, will you?" Anna Marie begged.

"Of course not," Jed said. He carried her as gently as a hurt child, putting her in the back of the wagon on the extra quilts they'd added in case the children wanted to nap in the middle of the afternoon.

"What happened?" The children all came running out of the water.

"The horse threw Anna Marie. I'm taking her home in the wagon. You kids mind Emma. I'll be back in an hour . . . or so," Jed said.

"Buster did it. Bad dog." Molly slapped the big dog on the hip.

"Buster didn't do it," Sarah whispered. "She jumped off the horse and fell down. I saw her. She can ride any horse around. Onliest thing she's good at. That's horse riding. She's just doing that so she can make Uncle Jed feel bad and make you mad, Emma."

"Well, it's working real well," Emma snapped. "Hey, I'm not mad at you kids, though. It's just that every time I turn around Anna Marie is there acting mean and spiteful."

"Yes, she is," Mary said. "She's just jealous because she's not as pretty as you. Let's go play some more. When Uncle Jed comes back it'll be time for dinner, won't it?"

"Yes it will," Emma said. She plopped down on the quilt and picked up her book. When the hour was finished she'd read three short stories and couldn't remember anything she'd read. The look of pure love on Jed's face when he held Anna Marie's tiny body next to him kept haunting her. Even if the girl was half witch and the other half pure mean, it didn't mean Jed didn't love her.

* * *

"Jed, darlin', I can't believe you married that big horse of a woman," Anna Marie whined, leaning into Jed on the wagon seat.

"Emma is not a horse of a woman. She's tall but that's not a sin, Anna Marie." Jed's hackles rose in defense.

"She's ugly." Anna Marie tilted her chin up defiantly.

"Beauty is in the eye of the beholder," Jed quipped. Whatever made him think he could ever spend a lifetime with Anna Marie, with her sharp tongue and whining. "You better scoot over. I'm all wet and you'll ruin your pretty blouse. Besides, you're engaged, Anna Marie, and it isn't proper."

"Proper," she said, giggling. "Well, this ain't proper either, Jed." She locked her left arm around his neck and cupped her right hand under his chin, twisting his face around until she could reach up and kiss him.

While her tongue teased his lower lip, he remembered the wedding kiss he and Emma shared. Kissing Anna Marie wasn't bad; right pleasant actually. But it sure didn't bring about the results that kissing Emma had done.

"Now tell me you don't love me," she said. "Tell me that you love that big ugly woman. Tell me you made a mistake when you married her, Jed Thomas."

"I won't tell you any such things," Jed pushed her gently to the other side of the seat. "Emma is my wife."

"But you can't love her. Good grief, she's just a hoyden and she's going to make all the girls like that. Out there half naked in the water. What can you be thinking about letting that go on, Jed?" Anna Marie huffed. If she couldn't win the war by attacking from one angle she'd try another.

"That's the newest fashion in bathing wear," he said, gritting his teeth. Next time Anna Marie could walk home.

"Sure it is. Your wife . . ." She dragged out the words like they were filth spewing from her mouth, ". . . is nothing but a gold digger. She probably was a bar maid or something like that and knew a good homestead when she saw it. You don't know anything about a mail-order bride, Jed Thomas. She's . . ."

"That's enough, Anna Marie. One more word about Emma and you can walk the rest of the way home."

She clamped her mouth shut and shoved her nose so high in the air that Jed might have laughed if he hadn't been so angry. Emma was not an ugly horse of a woman, and she wasn't a hoyden. So what if she was independent and talked about women's rights, voting and all that. She was still a lady and he loved her.

He moaned. Loved Emma. No, that wouldn't work. Not even if it could. Emma didn't love him. She didn't want to be married. Not ever. Jed sighed. He should have never tempted God by saying vows he didn't mean. Now, he'd fallen for the girl and there was absolutely nothing he could do about it because she could never love a farmer like Jed Thomas. Not a blue-blooded lady like Emma.

He delivered Anna Marie to the Elgin homestead, checked to make sure the horse had found its way home, and started back to the picnic. Misery rode in the seat beside him the whole way. By the time he parked the wagon under the shade tree, Emma was ready to run. Literally. Out of the whole territory and back to Crooked Oaks if necessary. She fought back tears of humiliation and disgust. Her insides were a mass of icy hot pure boiling rage at being treated like a child instead of a wife. Her heart kept telling her that she wasn't a wife, so Jed wouldn't even consider treating her as one. Her soul withered up like an old prune and died.

"Let's eat!" Jed called out to the children.

"So did she live?" Emma asked as she fetched the basket from the back of the wagon. "Did you have to carry her in the house or did she swoon again?"

"That's none of your business," he said. "It's done. I took care of it. No one is hurt. She'll be at church tomorrow beside her sister for the wedding."

"I'm the wife," Emma snapped.

"Only on paper," he retorted. "I read the telegram after I took her into the preacher's house. Beulah will be here on Tuesday. I'll ask Violet to bring her home when she goes to the train station to get her husband. I'm sure Violet will take you at the same time."

"I can hardly wait," Emma said.

"Wait for what?" Molly asked innocently.

"Nothing, sweetheart," Emma said, daring Jed with one look to say another word.

"Can I have a ginger cake if I eat all my chicken?" Molly asked.

"Yes, you can," Jed answered. "Matter of fact we're on a special picnic today, so you can have a ginger cake even if you don't eat all your chicken. Right, Emma?"

"Of course, Jed, darlin', whatever you say," she said in her best southern belle voice. But she didn't feel the empty endearments. She felt like feeding him pure poison. How dare he act like that. *Oh, well, two more days and it will be over. I'll go on to Enid and do what I set out to do in the first place. Make a way for myself. I don't need a husband any more than I need another hole in my head.*

Chapter Ten

Emma slept poorly that night. She'd raised the window but no breeze came through. Not one single little wispy wind to fluff the curtains. It had to be an omen, she figured as she lay rigidly on her side with her back to the bolster. The wind always blew in Oklahoma. At least that's what Violet said. From the blue northers in the wintertime that would chill a body to the bone marrow, to the hot summer wind that would do a job on a woman's face like a bake oven did on a trussed-up turkey. The only time the wind didn't blow was that few minutes before a tornado hit.

So was a tornado about to send them all scampering back to the root cellar again? She didn't think so. The moon was a bright white ball at the top of the window, rising above the house slowly. The stars were blinking like a million little lights. A physical tornado wasn't on the way to rip up the barn roof and hurt Buster again. It was an emotional one somewhere down in the bottom of Emma's soul. The time had come for her to go and instead of dancing on the moon with the stars as lights for her feet, her heart was a heavy stone in her chest.

She'd fallen in love with the children. Sarah needed dresses sewn up this summer; hers were too short. And besides, who was going to help her with math next school year? She'd confided in Emma that she wanted to go to college someday and be a lawyer. Now wouldn't that be something. A woman lawyer in Oklahoma. Emma would have a lot of work to do to make a way for that kind of liberal thinking.

Emma shut her eyes and saw Mary walking on the well. What would someone as elderly as Cousin Beulah do if she fell in the dark, deep well? The stunt had come nigh onto giving Emma a full-fledged case of vapors. Mary would do it again, just to test Beulah's mettle. A tear formed on the tip of Emma's heavy brown eyelashes. She loved Mary too much to think about her being hurt or perhaps even maimed for life.

Jimmy had two loose teeth and Emma would miss seeing him without them. She'd never know a shy hug from a six-year-old boy again. Not to mention all the hugs and cuddles from Molly, her baby. She even called her Mommy at the picnic that day. Emma's heart twisted into a knot and ached so badly, she could scarcely breathe.

And Jed, even with all his stubborn ideas about women, she loved him, too. Her eyes popped open so wide they hurt. Loved Jed. When had that happened? No, she wouldn't love him. It wouldn't do a bit of good if she did because he loved Anna Marie. Would always love that hateful witchy girl even when she was married to Alford. Emma shut her eyes tightly and willed herself to sleep.

It didn't work.

The next morning she was up before any of the rest of the family. She fried three chickens for lunch. A wedding at the church with a reception following. So very different from the weddings she'd attended in Georgia. Mostly they were planned for at least a year, then held in a ballroom with an elaborate dance following. That's what she would have had if she'd married Matthew. A six-month engagement. A wedding to rival any other wedding in Atlanta in the past twenty years, and the reception would have been lavish.

Things were different in the territory though. Simpler. Everyone would already be at the church, and few people could take a day from work to attend a wedding. Sunday was set aside for rest anyway, so a wedding and church picnic made all the sense in the world. Liberation in the first baby steps, she reckoned as she drained the chicken and put it in a crock bowl to set down inside the basket.

"Good morning." Jed came out of the bedroom, rubbing sleep from his eyes. "Is that chicken I smell?"

"Yes, it is. For dinner. We're having sausage gravy and biscuits for breakfast. By the time you get the cow milked it should be ready. I'll holler at the children in a few minutes." She avoided looking right at him. She didn't need to for one thing. She could see his dark green eyes below those thick almost black lashes, his hair that needed combing, and his bare feet poking out from the ends of his work pants with her eyes shut tight. She'd be able to see all of those things forever. When she was a hundred years old and sitting in a parlor of a tiny little house she'd remember the weeks she had in Oklahoma. The time when she exercised her own independence and fell in love. That was her comeuppance for saying vows before God that she would love, honor, and obey a man she didn't have any intentions of staying with until death parted them. It was a bitter dose but she'd just have to be woman enough to take it. She'd fallen in love with a man who could never love her in return.

Jed just nodded. No use for words. She'd do what was expected of her until Tuesday morning, then she'd shake off the Oklahoma dust from her feet and be gone. He wanted to cross the room in a few easy strides, take her in his arms, and kiss her just like he did that day they got married. Just to see if the stars burst into an array of brilliant colors again. But she'd made it clear she didn't want anything from Jed Thomas, except a little help and a ride back to town.

Later that morning as they sat together, one last time in church, Jed deliberately slid in close enough to Emma that he could touch her shoulder. The same jolt he always felt when he brushed against her was still there. Would probably always be there, even in his memories. He could never marry another woman now. Not since he'd fallen in love with his wife, even if it was too late. He'd have today and tomorrow and she'd be gone forever.

Emma shut her eyes and let the sensation of Jed's shoulder against hers rumble around in her body like a bullet in a rain barrel. She didn't care if he wasn't a fine southern gentleman with a multi-thousand acre plantation and an unlimited bank account to offer her. She ignored the preacher's sermon and let her mind wander. All the intrigue with the land rush had been her calling to come to Oklahoma. Her future awaited her in the new territory, but she'd botched the whole thing with her impetuousness. It was time to pay the fiddler and Emma hadn't even enjoyed the dance.

"Amen," Preacher Elgin finished the prayer. The children fidgeted in their seats, waiting to be let loose from the confinement. "And now it's time for a few minutes of recession. The wedding will be in thirty minutes. Children, remember you've got to come back inside for another ceremony, so no climbing the trees or running. That can wait until afterwards," the preacher said. "You are dismissed for thirty minutes."

"You look awful pretty this morning." Maggie Listen sidled up to Emma out on the lawn. "Jed did right good by getting you. Bet you can dance good, too."

"I hear you do a fine job on the dance floor," Emma smiled. At last, someone besides Violet was willing to make a step toward friendship. Even if it was Maggie, who everyone said was scarcely half-witted, and even if it was too late.

"Ah, I do all right, but dancing ain't never going to get me a husband like Jed Thomas. Anna Marie was about ready to pinch your head off, but she's just jealous. She had her eyes set on Jed, you know. But she didn't love him. She ain't going to love nobody much as she loves herself. There's lots of men in the territory. Not many women, though." Maggie kept whispering, casting glances toward Jed and three other men talking several yards away. "Alford tried to get me to go riding with him a few weeks ago. But he can't dance. I ain't marryin' up with someone who can't dance."

Emma smiled. Even Maggie Listen could tell what kind of substance Anna Marie had, so why couldn't Jed? Love was truly blind. And stupid, she added silently. "Well, Maggie, I suppose if you like to dance, then you'd better find a husband who won't step on your toes."

"That's the way I figure it," Maggie said. "There's Minnie, Anna Marie's oldest sister who got married last year. I got to go talk to her. See you later, Emma."

The church bell rang out in the hot Oklahoma morning, calling everyone back into the church building for a wedding. The Thomas family occupied the second pew just like always. Minnie took her place on the piano bench and played a lovely tune while everyone settled down and got ready for the wedding. The groom, a tall, lanky boy that didn't look a day over eighteen, followed Preacher Elgin to the front of the church. The young man standing beside him was his older brother. Both had the same straight, thin nose, full lips, and blond hair. They were dressed alike. Fine black broadcloth suits, brand-new and uncomfortable, but a man should make a few sacrifices for a bride like Sally.

He'd make Sally a good husband even if they were both young, Jed figured, sitting there beside Emma. *What makes you so knowledgeable on the subject?* His conscience stung him.

Maybe that's where he went wrong. He should have married when he was nineteen or twenty. Married the schoolteacher. He suppressed a chuckle. His teacher in Nebraska had been eighty years old if she was a day. She had thin gray hair that barely covered her scalp and a waistline bigger than a rain barrel.

Minnie struck a chord and everyone in the church stood for the bridal procession. Anna Marie appeared at the back of the church in a soft pink satin skirt and matching jacket. The bodice was styled with a peplum, accented with a belt that tied in a bow in the back, three-quarter sleeves with a wide flounce at the elbow, and a stand-up collar. Ecru lace trimmed the ruffle, the bottom of the peplum, and the collar. The skirt was worn with a bustle and had the same lace around the full bottom. Wildflowers were strewn through her dark hair and she carried a matching bouquet gathered up with a wide ribbon made of the same material as her dress.

She glanced at Jed, giving him a brilliant smile when she passed their pew. Emma bit her lip to keep back the tears and the tongue lashing she'd like to give the vixen.

A soft gasp filled the church when Sally stepped inside the doors. She wore a lovely altered version of the polonaise. The white satin bodice was fitted to Sally's tiny waist. Leg of mutton sleeves extended down to slim, fitted lace trimmed cuffs at her wrists. The panniers draped up at hip level to show off rows and rows of satin ruffles, each edged with pure white lace. Sally wore a full bustle and her petticoat was probably layered with ruffles to make the dress stand out like that.

Both creations had Violet's signature all over them. Emma would have to remember to tell her what a lovely job she'd done after the wedding. What kind of dress would she have chosen if she'd gotten married in Atlanta? Emma wondered as Sally slowly made her way to the front of the church where her groom waited. There were no answers because Emma didn't do what she was supposed to do. Strange, though, she surely didn't regret it. Not if it meant she had to be married to Matthew.

"Dearly beloved," the preacher intoned, reminding Jed of the words the sheriff had spoken. His thoughts went to the kiss he'd shared with Emma that day and the fact that sometime during the course of the past few weeks he'd fallen in love with her. He'd never tempt God again. That was a true vow. Not a pie-crust promise. Because when the promise had broken, so had his heart.

The sun was lowering, marking the end of the day when the Thomas family got home that evening. The children had romped and played with their friends. Mary held court under a shade tree and told the story of Anna Marie falling off her horse. All the little girls giggled, holding their hands over their mouths in derision. Even the children knew that Anna Marie could have stayed on the back of a bucking bull without losing a single hair pin. Jimmy chased off to the edge of Bear Creek to hunt for arrowheads or any other strange-looking rock. Molly clung to Emma, like always. Violet came to visit the quilt for a while and Maggie stopped by to tell Emma more Dodsworth gossip.

Emma was fitting in with the community. At last. Too late. It was the last time she'd see all the folks from the community. She missed them and she wasn't even gone yet. Would Maggie ever find a husband who would love to dance? Would Anna Marie ever grow up? Would Violet ever have children? Questions. Questions. Questions. No answers.

She carried Molly into the house while Jed and Jimmy unhitched the horses and put them away. Mary danced around in her new Sunday dress of green calico. Sarah declared she was hungry. Life went on at the homestead and would with or without Emma, she realized with a pang. In a couple of weeks, they'd barely remember what she looked like or that she'd made them all new clothing while she was there.

That night she brushed her hair while Jed flipped and flopped on his side of the bolster. So he couldn't sleep. Well, that was just fine with Emma. She lost count of how many strokes she given her long blond tresses and started all over again. She might as well brush until dawn because it was a cinch she wasn't going to sleep again that night. Or the next one either. Which was just as well. When she got on the train, she'd be so tired she'd sleep all the way to . . . where?

Where was Emma going after all? To Enid to begin a brand-new life? That didn't sound so inviting or exciting after all. No, Emma wanted to go home. Home to Atlanta where she knew the customs and the people. She'd told Jefferson she might come for a visit and he'd said she was welcome anytime.

"Are you ever going to get finished and blow out the lamp?" Jed asked testily.

"Shut your eyes," she snipped back at him.

"It doesn't block all the light," he said.

She set her jaw and stomped across the floor to the washstand. She cupped her hand over the globe of the kerosene lamp, leaned forward and with a puff, extinguished the light in the room. "Are you happy now? I can look at the stars and brush my hair at the same time."

"Thank you," he said tersely. Women were such unpredictable creatures. He loved Emma and couldn't tell her. It wasn't the light bothering him, but the sight of her sitting there in her snowy white gown with all that blond hair falling over one shoulder as she brushed it to a glistening shine. He wanted to brush her hair for her, push it all aside and kiss that tender skin on the nape of her neck, feel her shiver with delight at his touch. To do all that, Emma would have to love him as much as he loved her. He'd just have to learn to live with the fact that she could never love him, a simple farmer. Even though by territory standards he had a lot: a nice home, money still in the bank to build onto the house and buy more livestock, no mortgages, and he was improving the land so well he had no doubt that in five years he'd be granted the clear title to all of it. Yes, he had a lot, but he didn't have Emma's love.

The days of miracles were over.

"How are we going to tell the children?" she asked.

He sighed loudly. "I've been thinking about that. I'm going to tell them tomorrow night that you are going home to Atlanta to see your father and get the rest of your things. You'll be gone a couple of weeks and Cousin Beulah is going to take care of us while you are gone. In two weeks you'll have decided to stay a little longer, then a little longer. By the time school starts they'll all be used to Beulah and hopefully forget about you."

"Sounds like a good plan to me," she said, glad her back was to him so he didn't see the quiver in her chin. The children might forget her but she'd never forget them. Or Jed Thomas, either.

"Then that's the way we'll do it," he said.

"Jed?" It was on the tip of her tongue to ask if she might stay a while longer after Cousin Beulah arrived. But what good would that do? She'd still have to tell them all good-bye at some point and the longer she waited the more painful it would be.

"Yes, Emma?" He held his breath, hoping she would tell him that she'd realized she was in love with him after all. That she'd changed her mind about leaving.

"I want to thank you for what you've done these past weeks," she said. "Standing up to my father and Matthew for me. Marrying up with me when you didn't have to. Everything. You've been a real gentleman."

Grown men didn't cry, but if they did, he'd probably have shed enough tears right then to flood Bear Creek. "And you've been a real trooper. Good night, Emma," he said hoarsely.

"Good night, Jed," she said. One more time to say those

three words and then it would be over. The adventure. The independence. All of it. She'd go home to Crooked Oaks and be that crazy old maid everyone talked about. Only now she'd be a crazy old woman with a history.

Chapter Eleven

Breakfast was scarcely over when Violet drove her buggy up into the yard. Molly hadn't touched a bite of her pancakes and tears were streaming down her face. Sarah and Mary were quiet and Jimmy talked too much to cover up the uneasiness in the household. Jed just kept sneaking peaks at Emma, trying to memorize one last time every single detail about her. The way her aqua eyes turned darker when she was angry; the tilt of her chin when she listened to Molly begging to go with her; the faint smile when she looked at Sarah. All of it, because the lark was over. The promises, like pie crust, were broken. Emma's trunk was on the porch. Violet was waiting.

"Now, all of you come out in the yard and wave good-bye to me until you can't see me any more," Emma said, faking a cheerful attitude.

"Just two weeks?" Mary asked raggedly.

"Just two weeks," Emma lied. The whole experience had started with lies and now was ending the same way.

She carried Molly in her arms through the front door. Jed loaded her trunk in the buggy and shoved his hands into the pockets of his work pants. The time had come and he could scarcely bear the pain. He'd heard an old cliché quip, "Out of sight, out of mind." Emma would never be out of his mind or out of his sight. All he had to do was smell the sweet roses of summer and remember the soap she used to bathe at night. To look out the window at the stars and there she'd be brushing out that long, long blond hair in the moonlight.

"Well, are you ready?" Violet felt the heaviness of the situation. "The train will be there by the time we get to the station. I'll bring your cousin back, kids. Beulah? Sounds like a sweet lady to me."

"Not my Emma," Molly said around her thumb. "Come home my Emma in two weeks."

Emma didn't answer. She couldn't tell that sweet cherub another lie. Not if it meant she would lay down right there in the green grass and die. She just set Molly on the porch after a final hug and a kiss on her tear-stained cheek. "You be good for Cousin Beulah, Molly."

"Uncle Jed," Jimmy whispered out the side of his mouth. "Aren't you even going to kiss her good-bye? She is your wife."

Emma heard him and blushed.

Jed grinned. "Of course. I was just thinking about how much fun Emma will have in Georgia with her friends," he told Jimmy. He took two steps forward, folded Emma into a bear hug and then tilted her chin up for a kiss. A real one, like they'd shared on their wedding day. Only fitting somehow to start the whole thing off with a kiss and end it the same way.

The minute his lips touched hers, Emma felt her insides melt into a pile of trembling desire. If only he felt the same way she did, but happy endings were relegated to Kate's novels. In real life, the bride and groom didn't ride off into the sunset together and live happily ever after. In real life, the groom loved a woman he couldn't have because she was marrying another man very soon. The bride had fallen in love with the groom but she couldn't stay with him because that would be shackling him to a life of misery. Maybe her father had been right about marriage. Love shouldn't be involved in it at all. If that was the case, she should have married Matthew and made everyone else happy.

"Good-bye, Emma. Have a safe journey," Jed said past the lump in his throat.

"I will. Thanks again, Jed," she whispered in his ear, her soft breath making his heart beat extra hard.

"See you in two weeks." Jimmy began waving when Jed lifted her up into the seat. As if saying it would make it come true, because somewhere in his six-year-old heart he knew this was a final good-bye.

"Good-bye," she called as Violet slapped the reins against the horse's flanks. "Good-bye, good-bye."

When she couldn't see any of them any longer, she turned around and looked ahead. They passed the church and the creek while Violet hummed under her breath. Some little tune Emma didn't recognize. The future. That's what was ahead. Dim. Dull. No husband. No children. No love.

"So you want to talk about it?" Violet asked.

Emma shook her head, afraid to trust her voice.

"Okay, then just watch the countryside and remember where your heart is, Emma Thomas. Go visit, but come home to stay when you come back. Those children don't need their lives tore up," Violet said.

Emma nodded. No lies in the nod. She'd never come back.

Beulah was off the train and waiting in the station when Violet and Emma reached the station. She barely came to Emma's shoulder and was as round as she was tall. "Hello, you must be Violet, and you are Emma." Beulah looked up from the bench where she'd been sitting about five minutes. "Tell me, child, why are you leaving Jed?"

"It's a long story, Cousin Beulah. Please take good care of them. Molly is so insecure and needs lots of loving. I left the ironing all sprinkled and ready. But I put it in the spring house so it wouldn't sour so if you're too tired to tackle it today, it will still be fresh tomorrow. The dog will behave if you show it who's boss. Jimmy goes to the fields every day with Jed, but the girls . . ." Emma gushed.

"Not to worry, now girl," Beulah laughed. "I've taken care of folks all my life. Jed will explain it all, I'm sure."

"I'm sure he will," Emma said. "Thank you for coming so promptly. I'm going to buy my ticket now to go home. If anything should happen, Cousin Beulah, I'm at Crooked Oaks outside Atlanta."

"I'll remember that, child," Beulah said, as Violet's husband picked up her trunk and loaded it in the buggy. "You have a safe journey."

"Thank you," Emma said.

"What are you doing here?" Anna Marie said bluntly when Emma walked up to the end of the station to buy a ticket.

Emma jerked her head around. "What are you doing here?" she asked right back.

"I'm on my way to Enid to see about some special lace for my wedding dress," Anna Marie said. "It's almost ready. Violet has outdone herself. It's white satin like Sally's but instead of ruffles I'm having a train with layers of lace ruffles. A big bustle and tight-fitting sleeves. Where are you going?"

"I'm going home to Atlanta," she answered.

"Jed finally got wise and kicked you out, did he? Well, I knew he wouldn't keep something as big and ugly as you. Told him so last Saturday. You just ain't wife material. You might make a decent schoolteacher. Old maid schoolteacher. But there ain't nothing about you that Jed would want to look at every day forever," Anna Marie said, sniffing the air dramatically.

"You are surely honest," Emma said softly.

"He needn't think just because you're gone that I'll run right back in his arms. No siree. He made his choice and I might love old Jed Thomas, but honey, I'm not going to tie myself down to four brats. Alford can give me lots more than Jed. See my pretty ring." She held her hand out toward Emma. "And he's bought me a cute little house, too. I'm going to live in town. And any kids I raise will be my own, not some dead woman's."

"Well, good luck," Emma said. "I need to purchase a ticket to Atlanta, Georgia," she told the man behind the desk. "When does the next one going that way leave?"

"In about ten minutes," the man said. "You're in luck today, lady, because if you hadn't gotten here when you did, you would have had to wait all day for the next one going south."

"I don't think so," Anna Marie said, giggling. "If this had been her lucky day she wouldn't be here at all."

"How right you are." Emma looked down on the pretty girl. "Your ring is lovely. I hope you are very happy with Alford. Now I think I'll wait outside for my train."

"I'll be happy. Alford will see to that. I was a bit of a fool about Jed. Probably always will be. He's just so handsome and all. But he wouldn't have time to spoil me like Alford," Anna Marie smiled brightly.

Emma didn't answer. One more insult and the sheriff would put her in jail for wiping up the streets of Guthrie with the snit of a girl. Whether it made Emma's mother turn over in her grave or not. She'd endured as much of Anna Marie Elgin as she could stand for a whole lifetime. Getting away from her wicked barbs would be the very thing that kept her from shedding tears all the way back to Georgia.

The porter loaded her trunk for her. She took her place next to the window so she could watch the countryside speed past. She was a hundred years older than she'd been when she stepped off the train just a few short weeks before. She was now a married, probably soon-to-be divorced woman, not a young lady looking for independence.

Just before the train whistle blew, signaling only a couple of minutes before departure, a young man boarded in a hurry and entered the car where she was sitting. He looked around hurriedly and finally plopped down on the seat right across from Emma. For just a minute when she glanced toward him, she thought it was Jed. For a fleeting moment, she thought he'd come to take her back home. Back to the homestead where she belonged. When she looked the second time, she realized the man had dark hair and was tall, but his eyes were brown. It wasn't her handsome husband. Jed was probably dancing a jig around the barn by then. Singing to the top of his lungs and celebrating that the cross around his neck was finally broken.

"Mornin'," the man said. "Where you going?"

"Georgia," she answered, only a slight catch in her voice.

"Oh, my. I'm just going to Oklahoma City. Nearly missed the train. Got a business meeting down there. Political. We're going to be a state someday, you know?" he said.

"I'm sure. With congressmen and all of it," she smiled.

"Yes, we are," the young man said.

She watched as great chunks of land sped past the window. Emma's folly had come to an end. *Oh, no,* she thought. She had to make them stop the train right then. Even if she had to walk a couple of miles back to Guthrie. She'd forgotten something important. She'd given her word to Jimmy that she'd make cream puffs for him and she hadn't done it. She couldn't break her word.

But you did, her silly conscience said. *You broke your wedding vows so what's one little batch of cream puffs?*

Emma took her lace-trimmed handkerchief out of her reticule and began to cry. Silent tears dripping from her jawbone to the lapels of her bow Basque jacket that matched the traveling skirt of dark blue serge she'd made the week before. She'd never make Jimmy cream puffs. Never see him or Molly again. Or Sarah or Mary, either. Or Jed.

"Something I can help with?" the man asked.

"No. I just hate good-byes," she said honestly.

"Me, too," he said. "Well, I'm going to the dining car and see about some coffee. Have a good journey."

"Thank you," she said. Have a good journey? How many people had said that to her today? The journey was necessary but it couldn't ever be good, not when it separated her heart and soul from her body. Emma Maureen Cummins Thomas was on the way back to Atlanta to where she'd lived all her life. Her heart and soul were on a section of land in central Oklahoma Territory with Jed and four kids.

Jed laid on his cot in the tack room, laced his fingers behind his head, and stared at the rough beams in the ceiling. The smell of well-cared-for leather was all around him but he missed the sweet aroma of Emma's soap. Cousin Beulah had moved into their bedroom, took off her hat, and asked Sarah to go to the spring house and carry up the ironing. She took over the house with a steel hand and it looked like things were going to go right on schedule. At least everywhere but in his heart.

"Jed?" He heard rocks splatter on the wall of the barn. "Jed Thomas?"

"Emma?" He sat straight up, threw the bolster he'd stolen from the house into the floor, grabbed his trousers and jerked them on, forgetting about a shirt altogether. Emma had come back. She was outside and whispering for him. He stumped his toe on a bridle that had fallen from a nail in the wall, but he didn't even mind the pain. He and Emma would work something out.

"Jed, darlin'," Anna Marie rushed into his arms when he opened the barn door.

"Anna Marie? Whatever are you doing here?" Jed pushed her back.

"Coming to give you one more chance. My wedding dress is about finished. It can be for our wedding just as well as for mine and Alford's. I'll always love you Jed. Now that you've sent that big, ugly horse of a woman packing, we can get married. You can go to the courthouse and get a divorce next week, and I'll tell Alford I've always loved you. When it's final we can get married." She rested her palms on his bare chest. She'd show the whole community that she could have the man she wanted.

"Go home, Anna Marie. Just go home and marry Alford. He loves you and will make you a good husband. How did you know Emma was gone anyway?"

"I saw her at the station," Anna Marie pouted. "I can't believe you're treating me like this."

"Did she tell you she was only going home for a couple of weeks to get her things and visit her father?" Jed asked.

"No, I just figured you'd kicked her out." Anna Marie bit her lower lip.

"I didn't kick her out," Jed said honestly.

"Well, pardon me. You're going to be sorry someday, Jed Thomas. You're giving up the best woman in the world for you, and you know it."

"Emma?" Jed asked.

"No, you complete idiot. Me. I know you love me. When you picked me up on Saturday, I could see it in your eyes. Well, you've just sacrificed your last chance. She won't come back to you, Jed. When she gets to Atlanta, she won't come back to the territory for a dirt farmer. I heard in town that she was some kind of rich woman. Can't imagine why she married you to begin with if that's the truth. But the rich are crazy, Jed. Money makes them that way. I'm going home now. Don't you be telling that I came out here in the middle of the night. Alford would kill you dead. Want to give me one more kiss just for old time's sake?"

"No, I'm a married man," Jed told her. *Always will be,*

he thought. *I'll never divorce Emma. If she wants to marry that rich man, Matthew, then she can divorce me.*

Anna Marie jumped on her horse and rode bareback into the hot night wind, leaving only a giggle in her wake.

Jed went back inside the tack room, picked up the bolster and hugged it tightly, inhaling deeply of the scent on Emma's side. It would fade with time, but maybe if he closed his eyes, he would always be able to conjure up the scent that was Emma's alone. He arranged it at the edge of the cot, dropped his pants on the floor, and stretched out beside the bolster.

"Well, Emma, you've been on the train twelve hours now. Are you anxious to get home to your old beau? To your fancy plantation with all the money? I love you, Emma. Can your heart hear that all the way from mine to yours?"

Chapter Twelve

Emma awoke to the sounds of her father whistling out on the front porch. No breeze fluttered the sheer curtains on the windows in her massive bedroom. Just hot, summer sweltering humidity in Georgia. She was glad Jefferson could whistle and enjoy the morning. It was just another of many stretching in front of her like the endless grains of sand on a dry desert.

She threw back the sheet and pushed back the mosquito netting. A soft blue robe lay waiting on a rocking chair in the corner. The maid had already been in to refresh the water in the washbasin as well as her cut crystal pitcher with its matching drinking glass. Warm in the first; good cold well water in the second. She bathed her face and began the daily chore of getting dressed.

Tonight was the party. An engagement party. Her dress hung on the door of the big oak wardrobe in the corner of the room. Her father had insisted that she call the dressmaker and have something special done. She'd foregone fashion and designed the creation herself. Something reaching back in history to Napoleon's day. A French dress from the past, since she had no future.

She didn't awake in a festive mood even if the engagement seemed the best for everyone concerned. Her father surely was a changed man lately. Whistling all the time. Years had dropped from his face since she'd come back home, and then the engagement had made him even younger.

Emma nibbled at a bit of toast left on a tray with a pitcher of ice-cold tea. Nothing hot for her in the summertime. She didn't care if it wasn't good for her constitution to avoid hot tea in the morning. If she had to sip heat as well as be smothered by it, she'd simply die. She sipped the tea, faintly flavored with a bit of lemon. The house was already buzzing with preparations. She could hear the hum all the way up to the second floor where her suite of rooms was. Three rooms. The first one bigger than the whole bottom floor of Jed's cabin.

She stepped out on the balcony and sure enough, the gardeners were snipping here and trimming there, making the gardens beautiful. Red, white, yellow, and pink roses. Feathery soft white and pink azaleas. Petunias of every color in the world growing rampant. Marigolds spilling over the rock borders of the flower beds. Huge Boston ferns hanging on the verandah, their fronds waving, teasing that they had a wind blowing around them, when Emma felt nothing from her place on the second-floor balcony.

"It's a glorious day," her father singsonged up to her from the driveway when he caught sight of her. "Get dressed my daughter. It's a day for celebration."

"I'll be down shortly," she called to him.

With a heavy heart she made her way down to the ballroom where there was even more bustling than outside. Eulalie gave orders about where to place that silver candelabra, or that bowl of fresh cut flowers. Everything had to be perfect. After all, it was a time of celebration, as her father had said.

"Oh, Emma, I'm so glad you're here." Eulalie crossed the room in a no-nonsense stroll. "I need your help in the kitchen. Cook has the cakes all ready, but she says you've got a steady hand with that sugar icing. I've arranged the flowers for the top already and have them in the spring house to keep cool."

"I'll go right in," Emma said, grabbing an apple from the sideboard and biting into it on the way. Jimmy would have trouble eating apples right now because his two front teeth had to be gone by this time. She shook off the vision of a bright, smiling little boy with eyes like Jed and went to the kitchen. "I hear you need a hand with the icing," she said to the flustered cook.

"Do I ever. The cakes are all done but I just don't have the hand you've got. Your mother could make the icing perfect. Looked like a piece of artwork. Guess we shouldn't talk about her today, though, should we?" Edna, the cook, said.

"Don't know why not." Eulalie swept into the room. A force in anyone's sight even if she wasn't very tall. Just up to Emma's shoulder, a mop of chestnut-brown hair she kept in a tight bun at the nape of her neck and pecan-colored eyes. "She was a good woman and wife to Jefferson. This place doesn't need to go all hush-hush about her now. She was a part of the plantation for many years, and Emma can feel free to discuss her mother any time she wants."

"Thank you," Emma said. Eulalie was a refreshing soul and they'd become great friends in the weeks she'd been back in Atlanta.

"I need the shears to clip a few more roses. Found a gorgeous silver bowl hiding in the sideboard. Will look just wonderful on the foyer table," she said and was gone out the kitchen door before anyone could say another word.

"She's a force," said Edna, and laughed. "Breath of

spring this old place has been needing. No offense, Miss Emma."

"None taken. I agree with you," Emma said. She picked up a bowl and spoon and began to mix the cake icing. Her mother would have liked Eulalie. Both of them were no-nonsense women. They looked at life through the eyes of reality and didn't sugarcoat anything. So very different from most southern women.

One minute she was thinking of her mother and comparing her to Eulalie; the next she was looking across the table into Matthew's eyes. Now if that wasn't a contrast, she thought, letting the revulsion brew up from her toes to her snarling, pert nose.

"Good morning, darlin'," he said with a slow southern drawl. The voice was nice and if she shut her eyes she might be able to imagine that he was as handsome as Jed. However, she couldn't keep her eyes shut forever. The sun did come up every morning, regular as clockwork, and the thought of looking at him every day was enough to make her gag.

"Don't call me that," she said.

"Why not? You're going to marry me. It's a common endearment in this part of the world, Emma. I shall call you honey or sugar or darlin' forever." Matthew grinned but his eyes weren't smiling. They were evil.

"Matthew!" Jefferson followed Eulalie back into the house. "I'm so glad you're here. Emma, you be nice. This is a wonderful day and we don't need your sharp tongue making trouble." He laughed, hugging his daughter tightly to his side.

"Emma is a grown woman, Jefferson." Eulalie looped her arm through his. "And if she has something to say, she can do so. On that issue we'll have to disagree. Come in here and tell me if you like the way things are going."

"I'll love it, I'm sure." Jefferson let himself be dragged into the ballroom.

"I don't want any of your sharp tongue tonight, either," Matthew said.

"Then stay out of my way," she said, looking him straight in the eyes.

"When are you going to wake up?" he asked.

"My eyes are wide open," she said.

"No, they're not. They're shut to what you need to be doing, Emma. We will be married. I will be your husband and you will obey me," he said.

"On the same day I go ice skating in Hades," she retorted. "I've got work to do, Matthew. I want Eulalie's and Daddy's engagement reception to be perfect. They're having a simple ceremony with just me and her brother tomorrow morning. Don't let all this wedding and engagement affair make you think I'll finally give up and marry you. I've told you before, I am married already."

"That can be undone," he sneered. "A lawyer can take care of it. I don't like the idea of used goods, but I'll still marry you."

"I don't think it's got that cold down there yet." She glanced at the floor like she could see all the way to the flames of Hades.

Matthew stormed out in a sniff and Edna laughed. A rich laugh all the way from the bottom of her chest. Her big bosom shook. She wiped tears. She looked at Emma and the two of them started again. "That man is determined to have part of this land," Edna said. "He's a snake in the grass. Don't you ever listen to him. Rather see you die a woman with a history as marry up with that goat."

"Yes, ma'am." Emma's eyes twinkled for the first time since she'd gotten home.

Matthew stood across the room and watched Emma. She stood out, not only because of her height, but the dress was so different. A light aquamarine satin with an overlay of some kind of shimmery material. Fluid. She looked like she was wearing water with moonlight beams dancing on it. Eulalie's brother had been beside her all evening. A tall man in his middle thirties, from what Matthew judged. The same chestnut hair as his sister and the same light-brown eyes. Most likely a golddigger just like his younger sister. What could Jefferson be thinking about, marrying a woman that young? Eulalie was ten years younger than Jefferson. Just last week he was talking about the possibility of a son even yet. Said he still had a good number of years left in his body and he might have a son to leave Crooked Oaks to. He and Eulalie had discussed it and they both wanted as many children as the good Lord would bless them with. Laughter to fill the halls of the great house.

Matthew shuddered. Children. He'd tolerate them but to actually *want* a squalling red-faced baby to uproot his world? He and Emma would probably have a couple when she came to her senses, but maybe not. If Eulalie produced a male heir, Crooked Oaks would never be his. He could always live off the abundance just by being Emma's husband, but why would he need a child? If their union looked like it would produce an issue, then he would simply talk to the doctor in Atlanta. He smiled thinking of the damage he could do to punish Emma for marrying that dirt farmer.

Until then, he had to be a true southern gentleman. The future was a fog and Eulalie might produce a whole house full of stubborn girls just like Emma. Then he and Emma would have first rights to the plantation after all. He squared his shoulders at that thought and crossed the room in confidence.

"Good evening, Emma, you look lovely tonight. Is that the new thing out of Paris?" he asked.

"Of course not. It's the old thing out of Paris," she said. "But thank you, Matthew, for the compliment. If you'll excuse me I've promised this dance to Eulalie's brother. A fine man with an excellent mind. Did you know he's a doctor in New York City?"

"Of course I did. Did you know he's to be married in a few weeks?" Matthew lied.

"No, but whoever gets him will lead an interesting life," she said.

An hour later, Jefferson tapped on the side of his crystal water glass with the edge of a sterling silver spoon. Silence filled the great hall as he led Eulalie to the staircase and the two of them climbed halfway up. She wore a dress of flowing copper silk, styled somewhat like Emma's only with leg of mutton sleeves. The bodice plunged to show her ultra-white chest and stopped before even a discreet amount of cleavage could be displayed.

"Friends and neighbors, Eulalie and I are glad you have joined us on this wonderful occasion. This is the formal announcement of our engagement, but it's not a long engagement. Tomorrow morning, we will be married in a private ceremony right here at Crooked Oaks. As you all know it's the wrong time of year for a honeymoon with the cotton crop in the stage it's in, so we'll be at home for visitors after Sunday. Please feel free to stop by and visit us. Eulalie is from southern Louisiana and she'll be glad for the friends. Have a good time now." He drew Eulalie to his side and hugged her tightly.

"A toast." Emma raised her punch cup. "To many happy days at Crooked Oaks with Eulalie as mistress. I would have run away and eloped years ago if I'd known that's what it would take to wake Daddy up."

The crowd snickered and Jefferson smiled. Eulalie mouthed the words "Thank you" to Emma and beamed.

"A lovely toast," Matthew said at her side. "Come outside and draw a breath of fresh air with me, Emma. It's stifling in here with all the candles. There's not a breeze to be bought between here and the Gulf of Mexico."

"No thank you," she said.

"Hey, I won't bite you. I'm just asking for a few minutes of your time on the verandah. We'll drink punch and sit in the chairs. I won't even ask you to walk in the shadows with me."

"Oh, all right," she agreed. Maybe, just maybe, she

could convince him once and for all that she wanted absolutely nothing to do with him.

"See there. I have no vampire teeth." He smiled when they reached the verandah. "Shall we sit?"

"No, Matthew, I don't want to sit with you. I came out here to tell you that . . ."

"Don't, Emma. Let me speak my piece first. I know you ran away because you felt pressured to marry me. I know you don't love me. I also know you married that man and now you are damaged goods. You will never find a husband. No southern gentleman wants another man's castoffs. You didn't come home for a visit. You came home because that dirt farmer didn't want you. Face it, woman. You're too tall. You've got a bad temper and you have no idea when to shut your mouth. I'm willing to work on all of it and give you a respectable name. You can divorce the man next week. By the time the papers are finalized we can get married. The only thing is I won't wait for the wedding night, Emma. You are already a soiled dove so why should I wait? That will be my consolation prize for giving you respectability."

"You are disgusting." She snarled her nose and turned her back on the man.

He reached out and grabbed her arm, spun her around with more strength and force than she could ever imagine he'd have. "You will do what I say." His voice was filled with hate and anger. "Do you understand me? No more riding that hoyden bicycle up to the lake. No more sitting for hours reading those filthy books. I'm going in there now and tell your father you've agreed to the divorce. He'll be elated."

The man was out of his mind. The devil was jumping around in his eyes and his grip was hurting her. Tomorrow she'd have bruises on her arms to show his mean, hateful attitude. She pulled away from him, only to feel the sting of his palm across her cheek.

"I'll tame you or die trying. After the party, I will knock

on your door. You will open it to me. Do you hear me, woman?" he asked.

Emma tried to jerk her arm free but he gripped all the harder. She raised her other hand to slap him and he caught it midair in a vice-like grip. He was deranged, a mad spider who had to be smashed. She stomped the instep of his right foot and kicked him as hard as she could in the left shin.

He dropped to his knees and moaned. At that time Jefferson and Eulalie's brother, Jackson, stepped out of the ballroom onto the verandah.

"Matthew, are you proposing to my married daughter?" Jefferson laughed.

"No, Daddy, he's being a perfect fool. He's demanding all kinds of ugly things from me. Telling me to divorce Jed and that I have to let him in my bedroom tonight. He says I'm a soiled dove and damaged goods," Emma said. She felt her cheek; it was still burning from his vicious right-hand slap.

"She's lying," Matthew said. "She begged me to marry her. To give her another chance. When I said I didn't love her she turned mean and kicked me."

Jefferson removed her hand and the fiery imprint of the man's hand shined in the light flowing from the ballroom. "Did she slap herself?" he asked.

Matthew stood as straight and tall as he could. "I'll be leaving now. Jefferson, I hope this little altercation won't make you change banks."

"This little altercation?" Jefferson touched his daughter's face and noticed the red handprints on her arm. "Matthew, don't you ever set foot on Crooked Oaks again. If you do I'll kill you. That's your only warning. Emma, honey, go in the house with Jackson. To the kitchen. We'll put some ice on that cheek and you can enjoy the rest of the evening. I'll be at the bank next week, Matthew, to move all of my accounts somewhere else. You are despicable. A blight to southern gentlemen."

"She'll never find a husband. She's just an ugly overgrown hateful girl," Matthew said, trying to save a little of his dignity. He'd be fired from his job if Jefferson told the president of the bank why he was moving his accounts.

Jefferson's fist answered him and Matthew found himself laying on the dirt, trying to convince his lungs to suck up some of the humid night air. "That's my daughter. I don't abide such filth from any man about her. Get off my land. Don't you ever let me see you again. She was smarter than me all along. She could see what a rogue you were from the beginning."

"Thank you, Daddy." Emma looped her arm through his and with Jackson following them, she led him back to the party. "You go dance with Eulalie. Jackson, I think that Carolina Prescott has her eye set on you if you're not spoken for up in New York."

"No ma'am, I am not," Jackson smiled. "And Carolina is a fine-looking young lady. I just love that southern accent of hers."

"You all right, Emma?" Jefferson asked seriously.

"I am now, Daddy. I'm just fine. Haven't been better in weeks and weeks. I'm going in the kitchen until this handprint goes away and then I'll join you all."

"I apologize for my lack of judgment." Jefferson kissed her gently on the red cheek. "It won't happen again. You're a grown woman, Emma. I'll abide by your decisions about your life. And honey, I won't ever threaten to cut you out of my will again. I love you, Emma."

"I love you, Daddy," she smiled. "Eulalie is waiting for you. Go on. It's your party. Not mine. Now get."

Emma applied a cool cloth to her red face and leaned against the doorframe. If she'd married Matthew in the beginning she would have had a miserable life. So her impetuousness hadn't been for naught after all.

"Oh, Jed, why don't you come riding up on a white horse and take me back home where I belong?" she said to the dark room.

Chapter Thirteen

Beulah took the last six quarts of green beans from the boiling water bath. She'd canned sixty quarts since the first picking. She'd canned beans, blackberries, and peaches and put up a few jars of pork when Jed shot a wild hog. They'd pickled a good portion of the pig, sinking it deep in a special sauce her husband had taught her to make.

"When's my Emma coming home?" Molly played with the button box in the middle of the living-room floor. It was the only thing that kept her occupied for hours on end while Beulah and the older girls kept the house going. It was also a question she asked every single day.

"Later, baby girl. Later," Beulah said.

"She's not coming back," Sarah whispered to Beulah. "She's been gone forever. Ever since the first of summer and we'll be going to school in another month. Something has happened to her, Aunt Beulah. I just know it."

All three chins wiggled when Beulah shook her head.

148

The children were smarter than Jed gave them credit for. He had explained the situation to Beulah the second day she was at the homestead. She could see the anguish in his eyes when he spoke the woman's name even then, and it hadn't dulled one bit since.

"Well, we got beans to pick again today. And the iceberg radishes are ready to pull up. Then we'll turn the soil over real easy and plant another go of radishes. Maybe red ones this time. Can't let the ground lay fallow when there's mouths to feed." Beulah dragged out a soup pot and dumped a jar of venison in it. A nice hot stew for supper would make them all forget Emma.

How could they forget? she asked herself. Every time one of them put on a dress, they remembered she made it for them. When Jimmy found a can of ginger cakes behind the sewing machine, they talked about how Emma said they'd be good until Christmas, if they lasted that long. Scarcely a day went by that her name wasn't mentioned a dozen or more times.

"Hello," a woman's voice called from the front porch.

"Come right in," Beulah yelled back. Violet! Thank goodness for some company on that Saturday afternoon. "Got time for a glass of cold buttermilk?"

Violet opened the door and nodded. "Clabber would be even better."

"Sarah, you and Mary run out to the spring house and bring in that gallon we've got setting up. Sit, Violet. Prop your feet up and tell me what's going on in town. Is anybody doing anything other than canning green beans and planting radishes right now?" Beulah asked.

"Nothing much else is there. Menfolk is praying for rain. I'm sewing fast and furious as I can. Somedays I feel like I been chained to that treadle sewing machine. And I still can't keep the dressmaker in stock from one Tuesday 'til the next. Reckon we could talk?" She raised an eyebrow to let Beulah know she had something to say that the children shouldn't hear.

"Sure, in a few minutes," Beulah said. Company wasn't an everyday affair so she couldn't cheat the kids out of their time with Violet.

"Did you hear about Anna Marie?" Violet asked with a nod about the other business.

Mary's ears picked right up as she set the gallon jar of clabbered milk on the cabinet and watched Beulah shake it well before pouring up a tall glass for herself and Violet. "Yuk," Mary said. "Do all old people drink that stuff?"

"Of course," Violet laughed. "Once you get twenty years old, you just wake up one morning and you realize you're old. Your body says give me some clabber. Good old cold clabber because I am old. Just wait, Mary. It'll be here before you know it."

Mary giggled. "You're not old, Violet."

"I must be. I'm drinking clabber, but I bet Anna Marie isn't drinking clabber this morning. She's expecting a baby," Violet whispered to Beulah. "Sick as a weak kitten every morning, Sally told me. She beat Sally and Minnie to the cradle. Her mother is crowing about being a grand-mother, and Preacher Elgin has a brand-new spring to his step. Bet he's got visions of a hunting buddy after raising up three girls," Violet said.

"Times sure have changed. In my day a girl didn't tell something like. She kept it hid until she had to go into confinement. I guess with that Susan Anthony and her co-horts things begin to change," Beulah said. "I can't see that spiteful child as a mother."

"That's what I thought, but I guess she's going to be whether she wants to be or not. It's too late to go back and change her mind now. Was a pretty wedding a couple of months ago, wasn't it?" Violet said.

"Yes, it was," Beulah said. "You outdid yourself on them dresses. Never did see anything prettier than the one Anna Marie wore. She looked like an angel."

"Too bad she don't act like one," Mary laughed. To be included in the grownup talk was exhilarating. Wait until

Sunday when she gathered her friends around her and told them Anna Marie was going to have a baby. She fidgeted with the excitement.

"Why don't you girls take Molly and take a hike up to the fields. I bet your Uncle Jed would just love to have the rest of that jug of clabber to help him make it until dinnertime," Beulah said. "Take two glasses just in case Jimmy is feeling real old today."

"But we want to stay and listen," Mary protested.

"I want to go see Jed," Molly declared, standing up and reaching for Sarah's hand. "Let's go."

"Oh, all right," Mary said. "But we're coming right back."

Beulah waited until she could see them going across the backyard and up to the place where Jed was plowing. Then she turned to Violet with a question in her bright blue eyes set in beds of ancient wrinkles.

"I got a letter from Emma," Violet said. "I had to come tell you about it. She told me all about her father getting remarried to some woman ten years younger than him. She hopes they'll have a son to carry on the Cummins name and to be an heir to the plantation. Says she really likes the new stepmother."

"Did she ask about them?" Beulah nodded toward the back of the house.

"Yes, she did. Were they well? Had Anna Marie really married Alford? Everyone by name in the whole church and community, even Maggie Listen. But not about Jed," Violet said.

"Then that's who she wants to hear about the most and is fearful of asking," Beulah said with a twist to her thin lips. "She's pining after him or she wouldn't be writing to you. I told you she'd not be able to stay gone long. I could see the look in her eyes."

"She didn't mention ever coming back, Beulah," Violet said. "Said she stayed busy on the plantation. She and her stepmother, Eulalie, were working on a new flower garden.

She did say she and her father had come to an understanding after that horrid man, Matthew, was mean to her."

"Lawsy, Jed would die if he knew a man had mistreated her. Did she say what she meant by mean to her?" Beulah's eyes opened wide.

"Said they'd had an altercation and the man slapped fire out of her and bruised her arm to boot, but she said she kicked him in the shin. Her daddy put him going and I guess he got fired at the bank the next week too. He'll be madder than a grizzly with a sore tooth. She'd better stay away from him, I'm thinking," Violet said.

"Well, Jed is moping around like he's lost. Nary a day passes that the children don't ask about her or mention her name. I'm ready to take matters into my own hands, I just tell you. I'm going to think on it for a couple of days, but on Tuesday when you go get your husband, why don't you just swing by here. I may need a ride to the train myself. Jed Thomas has it too easy. If things were a mite harder for him, he just might send for her or better yet go get her."

"With four kids. Can't you just see Jed and all them kids showing up at the door of that big mansion down there? It's a muddle for sure, Beulah. If I'd known then what I know now, I wouldn't have taken her to the train or brought you back." Violet finished the glass of cold clabbered milk.

"If I'd known what I know now I would've never left Texas. Thank goodness I didn't sell my place until I saw if this is what I wanted. I'm telling you, we got to do something, Violet. You just come on by here on Tuesday. I'll figure out something by then."

Beulah fretted for two days. She prayed about it in church and gave an extra offering when the plate was passed. Surely God would give her a sign of what she should do before Tuesday. She ate so little Jed asked if she was sick on Sunday night and she snapped at him. She retired to her room, leaving the supper dishes for the rest of the family to take care of. She did the laundry on Monday because that's what she was supposed to do, but her heart wasn't in it.

"I'm going home," she announced after supper that evening. "I don't like it here. It's too much work for a woman my age and besides I miss my friends and town living."

"But Cousin Beulah," Jed sputtered.

"I'm leaving tomorrow morning. Violet is picking me up and taking me back to the train station," she said bluntly. "You and these children made it through six months without a woman to take care of you all, so you'll survive, Jed. Sarah and Mary are good help in the house and everything will work itself out."

"But couldn't you stay a week! I'll hunt for a housekeeper. Maybe Violet knows a woman in Guthrie willing to work for me and keep the children," he begged.

She almost relented. She'd never felt more alive than she did with the children all around her. But she held her ground and shook her head. "Nope, I'm going tomorrow morning."

"Is my Emma coming home when Violet takes you to the train?" Molly asked.

"I don't know," Beulah said firmly and went to her room, where she spent the rest of the evening packing her things behind closed doors.

Jed's world crumbled around him in a million pieces. They'd be going back to the time when Molly went with him to the field because Sarah and Mary couldn't take care of housework and her, too. He'd come in late and fix supper, get up early and make breakfast. The children would help. But what had come over Beulah? She hadn't been her usual jolly self since Violet came to visit last weekend. Then the two of them had their heads together on Sunday like conspiring nine-year-old girls. Now this. He could have pitched a tantrum like Molly if only it would do a bit of good.

"Okay, kids, you heard Cousin Beulah. Tomorrow morning we change up the way we do things again. We can make it. We did before . . . before Emma." He said the word for the first time in months, even though he'd heard it every day and it was engraved in indelible ink on his heart.

"Can we wave good-bye like we did when Emma went away? Is Violet going to bring her home to me?" Molly asked.

"I don't think so this time," Jed said. He'd been a fool to think they'd forget her in a few weeks. If anything they'd made an idol of her. But then that wasn't hard to do. Emma had done everything so effortless and perfect, it was easy to think of her as an angel with big fluffy white wings and a golden halo. Sometimes he had to remind himself of the arguments they'd had. Of her stubbornness and independence. She was probably sitting on the White House lawn right now demanding an audience with the President himself. If she got through the front doors, women would be standing in line to vote at the next election, because even the President of the United States of America was no match for Emma.

"When?" Molly demanded an answer.

"Maybe before school starts." Jed put her off but his voice didn't sound very convincing.

Beulah listened to the conversation through the door and stuffed her chubby hand in her mouth to keep from giggling. She'd only played matchmaker one other time and it had had a wonderful outcome. She'd plotted with her late husband to get his sister and her brother together. They celebrated their thirtieth wedding anniversary just last year. Beulah would be long gone and dead by the time Jed and Emma celebrated their thirtieth anniversary, but it was forthcoming. Violet said Emma loved Molly more than life. So Beulah would use that to bake the matchmaking cake.

"Uncle Jed, I haven't ever ironed before. We just wore the clothes without ironing them, remember? Then Emma started making them all nice," Sarah said.

"We'll manage," Jed said firmly.

Beulah's shoulders shook. Let them manage. They were spoiled rotten, and he'd never do one thing if she didn't leave. Not one solitary thing. Just go to the fields and get old as Methuselah, living on memories. Beulah Thomas was a woman of action, not one of those weeping willows. She'd fought off attacking Indians when she and her husband were settling their property. She'd lived through raids, grasshoppers, drought, floods, you name it. Texas was every bit as unyielding as Oklahoma, and suddenly she yearned for her own home. Even though she'd thought she was ready to leave it, she wanted to go home. She'd lived in Texas all her married life. She wasn't leaving it again. She'd die in the hot, dry west Texas desert land.

The homesickness was the sign she'd been praying for. Yes, Beulah was doing what was right. God had visited her with a blessed sign, just as surely as he'd given Elijah one in the old testament. Jed Thomas would thank her in thirty years, even if she wasn't around to hear him.

The next morning after breakfast Violet drove up in the yard. Beulah met her at the front door. She had her best Sunday blue dress on and her hat tied firmly under her chin. There was a twinkle in her eyes but Jed absolutely looked stricken. He felt like the weight of the whole world was upon his young shoulders.

"Morning, Jed. Children." Violet nodded. "Going to be another hot one."

"Yes, it is," Jed said. "Could sure use some rain."

"Bet we don't get it. Don't often rain in July in Oklahoma," Violet said. "Just hope the wells don't run dry. Stay out of the creek. It's just an invitation for the cholera, but I don't have to be tellin' you about that, Jed. Reckon you better get those valises and her trunk in the buggy. The train will be there by the time we make it to town. I think the southbound leaves pretty quick this morning. If we're late she can't leave until evening," Violet said.

"Good-bye children. Give me a hug and listen to your Uncle Jed. Be good little children like you've been when

I'm here. No walking on the well, Mary. Promise?" Beulah cupped Mary's face in her chubby hands.

"I promise. It would make you and Emma both sad if I fell in." Mary wiped away a tear. "Good-bye, Aunt Beulah. Will you write to me?"

"Yes, I will. Violet can look for the mail when she goes into town once a week. And when you get old enough you can ride the train to Texas and spend a month with me. That is, if Uncle Jed can spare you. One at a time, but not all together. One kid at a time is enough for an old woman like me," Beulah said, hoping that would make the parting easier. In a few weeks, they wouldn't be wanting to leave the homestead. Not if her plans worked out.

"You mean it?" Sarah asked, wide-eyed.

"Sure, I mean it," Beulah said. "Now wave to me until I'm gone. You're a lovely family. Maybe Uncle Jed will get you an aunt someday to live here."

"He did. My Emma," Molly smiled. "She's coming home, Aunt Beulah. I know she is."

"I hope so, Molly." Beulah kissed her sweet little cheeks.

"So you think he'll go get her?" Violet asked when they were out of sight of the house and well on their way to Guthrie.

"Nope. Stubborn male pride. He doesn't think he's good enough for a fine southern lady. Good looking. Hard working. But more stubborn than a mule my husband bought one time. Crazy animal couldn't be trained for nothing. Finally sold him. That's Jed Thomas. Acts just like his father who was my daddy's first cousin. Nope, he won't go after her. But I think I know how to fix that little problem," Beulah said.

"Oh?" Violet raised an eyebrow and flicked the reins to make the horses go faster.

"Yes, and it's going to work, because I got a sign from the Lord last night. I been praying and praying for something to tell me I was doing the right thing running off and leaving that little family in the lurch like that. Well, there

I was worrying my head off when a vision of my house in Texas and all the times me and my late husband had there come to mind. Seemed like I was pining for home. That was my sign, Violet. He was telling me to go home. He'll take care of Jed and the kids. But I have to help Him just a little bit more, so you take me by the telegraph office before we get to the train station. Better hurry up those horses if I'm going to make that southbound train this morning. Texas is calling my name."

"Yes, ma'am." Violet flicked the reins again.

Beulah went into the telegraph station and was back in the buggy in just a few minutes. Violet asked her what she'd sent but she just laughed, saying that the less Violet knew in the next few days the better off she'd be. When the fireworks started it would be best if Violet was completely innocent. She'd shoulder the whole thing by herself.

"Okay," Violet laughed. Let the old girl have her day of glory. If whatever she did produced the end product they all wanted, then it would be worth it all. Jed looked so forlorn that he just about made her weep.

It wasn't until recently that Violet realized Jed Thomas was pining for Emma. Last Sunday one of the children mentioned her name and Jed's face lit up like a bunch of stars on a cold night. He was in love with his own wife and Violet would bet dollars to cow patties he'd never told her so. Emma had confided the real reason they were married to her that last day when they were on the way to the train station, and the pain in her voice let Violet know she was in love with Jed and thought it was too late.

"Oh, the way the world does turn," Violet mumbled as she put Beulah on the train and waited for her husband to bring in the next northbound engine.

Chapter Fourteen

The mosquitoes were as big as buzzards and even the netting couldn't keep them at bay. Emma swatted at one buzzing around her ears but missed the critter. She couldn't go back to sleep and dawn peeped through the window anyway. She could hear bustling in the kitchen. Jefferson and Eulalie were both early risers. She'd join them for breakfast this morning.

She threw back the thin sheet and pushed the netting aside. She chose a batiste dress with embroidered red roses around the hem, and a simple petticoat. No corset on a sweltering hot day like today. She pulled her hair back in a tight knot at the nape of her neck, securing every errant strand with hair pins. Before noon it would be scraggling down and plastering itself to her forehead, neck, and cheeks with pure old sweat. A smile tickled the corners of her mouth at that thought. Ladies didn't sweat. They had vapors if it got too warm but they didn't sweat.

"How did a misfit like me get born into Southern society?" she asked aloud as she descended the winding flight of stairs to the main floor. "Taller than lots of men and I sweat."

"Who are you talking to, dear?" Eulalie asked from the bottom of the wide staircase.

"Myself," Emma said. "Good morning to you. Looks like we're in for another hot July day. Daddy in the dining room?"

"Yes, I was just joining him. You are up early. Going to share breakfast with us this morning?" Eulalie looped her arm in Emma's and threw open the dining-room doors.

"Well, well," Jefferson said, smiling. "My two best girls together for breakfast. A fellow couldn't ask for more than that on a fine July morning."

Edna set a platter of scrambled eggs topped with bacon bits on the sideboard with the silver coffee service and a huge silver bowl of fresh fruit. "Mornin' Emma. Surprised to see you down this early. Oh, I forgot. There's a note for you on the sideboard in the foyer, Man brought it out just a few minutes ago. Said it came to the telegraph office late last evening and he couldn't leave right then. I didn't get the wherefores and whyfores but he was in a big hurry."

"A telegram?" Emma's face was a puzzle.

"Probably from that scoundrel, Matthew," Eulalie said. "I heard he went to Philadelphia. He's most likely begging you to join him."

Emma laughed out loud. "There's lots of rich women in Philadelphia. He can find another one. It's just that he won't get Crooked Oaks with any of them. If you'll excuse me, I think I will find out who is sending me a telegram."

She found the folded note on the silver slaver on the credenza and opened it. Her heart raced as she read the short message:

Molly very sick stop maybe dying stop come quickly stop Beulah Thomas

"Daddy," she yelled from the foyer. "Eulalie, I've got to go to Oklahoma."

"Whatever are you talking about?" Jefferson's tall frame filled the doorway into the dining room. "What did that telegram say?"

"Oklahoma?" Eulalie frowned.

"It's Molly. You remember Molly, Daddy. The little girl who hid in my skirt tails and sucked her thumb. She's ill and may be dying. I've got to go. Please understand," she said.

"Of course we understand," Eulalie put her arm around Emma's quivering shoulders. "Come on, I'll help you pack a trunk. Jefferson, call someone to take her to the train station. You'll need a companion."

"No, I went once by myself and I came home by myself. I don't need a companion. I just need to hurry. What if she's . . ." Emma couldn't make herself say the word or picture Molly dead.

"She'll be fine until you get there and you'll take care of it when you do." Eulalie patted her arm. "Jefferson, get us a buggy and a driver. Emma will be ready to go in half an hour."

"But you can't go back there," Jefferson said. He remembered the size of the cabin. Squatter's houses were bigger than that. And the calluses on her hands when she came back to Crooked Oaks. They were barely healed after all these weeks. "I'll send a telegram back to Guthrie and tell the sheriff there to send the best doctor they've got out to take care of Molly and to send us daily reports on her. You don't have to go back there to that forsaken place."

"Yes, I do, Daddy," she said. "Molly needs me or Beulah would have never sent the telegram."

"Promise me you'll come home in a couple of weeks?" He hugged her tightly.

"No, I won't promise anything ever again if there's the slightest chance I can't keep the promise. I lied to Molly, telling her I'd come back. I lied in front of witnesses and even God when I married Jed. If Molly needs me, I'll stay until she's well or . . ." She stumbled over the words and tears gathered on her long lashes.

"Don't get maudlin," Eulalie said. "We've got things to do."

By mid-morning Emma was on a train, sitting next to the window, watching Georgia fade away. She alternately prayed that Molly wouldn't die of the cholera because that's what she decided the child must have, and berated herself for ever leaving the poor baby in the first place. She tried to read Kate's stories to make the time go faster and take her mind off what she might find in Oklahoma. It didn't work. Novels were fine but Emma had grown up in the past few months. Life wasn't a storybook. Happy endings weren't guaranteed.

When the train reached Dallas, Texas, she considered sending a telegram asking Jed to meet her at the station. But if Molly was taking her last breath, she couldn't ask him or Beulah to leave her. No, she'd just fend for herself. She could rent a buggy or maybe she'd connect with Violet. No, that wouldn't work either. Violet went into Guthrie on Tuesday and Friday mornings.

By the time the train stopped in Oklahoma City, Emma was a basket of two days' worth of frayed nerves and worry. Less than an hour and she'd be in Guthrie and then she'd know if she was too late. Jed said that Joy and Billy died in less than forty-eight hours and Molly was just a little wisp of a thing.

"Well, lookee who come back to the wilderness from the big city." The sheriff was the first person she saw when she went inside the train station.

"Sheriff," she nodded respectfully.

"Am I going to have to marry you and Jed up again today?" he teased.

"Don't think so, sir. You heard any news from the homestead? How's Molly?" She held her breath as she waited for the answer.

"Just heard that elderly woman he had out there helping him up and went back to Texas. Couple of days ago. Haven't heard why. Something wrong with Molly? She one of them kids Jed is trying to raise?"

"The baby. About three years old," Emma answered. "Good day, Sheriff. I've got to get the livery and hire a rig."

"Good day to you to, Mrs. Thomas." The sheriff tipped his hat.

Her skirt swished almost as loudly as the noise inside her head, plaguing her as she hurried toward the livery stable. It must be cholera and it scared Beulah away. That meant Jed was out there with four children, maybe four sick children, trying to keep up the homestead and take care of them at the same time. What if? She shook the morbid picture of four little graves beside their parents under that big pecan tree in the middle of the property.

"Mrs. Jed Thomas," John Whitebear called out to her from the general store's front door. "Where are you going?"

"To the livery stable to rent a buggy or hire someone to take me home," she told him.

"I'm going that way. Brought a wagon to take home supplies. I'll take you if you don't mind going with a bunch of Indians." His brown face lit up when he grinned.

"I'd ride with the devil to get there," she said. "When are you leaving?"

"Right now. I was on my way to the wagon. We brought three wagons to take supplies. I don't think we'll drive as fast as the devil, but I bet we can get you there before dinnertime." He motioned to the wagon piled high with supplies.

"You think we could find room for a trunk and a couple of valises?" she asked.

He nodded. "At the train station?"

"Yes, on the dock, waiting," she answered.

True to his word, John delivered her to the front door of the homestead at a few minutes before noon. She shouted a hello while John unloaded her trunk and luggage on the front porch, but got no response. Cold chills chased down her backbone and she shielded her eyes with the back of her hand so she could see farther out into the fields.

"Looks like Jed and the kids aren't home right now," John said.

"You go on. You've got a ways to go, and I'll wait," she said. "Thank you so much for your help, Mr. White-bear. You really must bring your wife and kids to meet me someday soon. Maybe we could plan a picnic and swimming party before our school starts." She tried to be amiable but her heart was beating so fast she could hear every thump in her ears.

"I'll tell Bessie you said that. She'd be honored and pleased for a day of play. Tell Jed I said hello and to keep his squaw at home. Or at least to be home when she gets here," he said, laughing as he drove away.

Emma went inside the house to find the breakfast dishes still on the table. Five plates and glasses with dried milk inside. Everyone was at least well enough to eat. Unless there was other folks here for a funeral. The stove was stone cold and the floor needed sweeping. The door to the bedroom was wide open and the bed was unmade. Strange, but the bolster still separated the bed into two different halves.

Giggles. Emma heard giggles coming from the back of the house. If Mary was walking on the edge of the well again, she was going to make her sit until suppertime. Emma shuddered. If Mary was alive she intended to smother her face with kisses and forget about punishment. She ran to the back door to see three little girls chasing through the high grass toward the house. Three for sure. She counted them. Sarah. Mary. Molly. All running and giggling in spite of the horrid Oklahoma heat.

Emma sat down with a thud in the rocking chair and waited. They tumbled in the back door, Molly first declaring she'd won the race. Sarah next, telling them both they had to get the dishes done and the floors swept before Uncle Jed got home that evening. Mary arguing that they could play for a while, then work.

"My Emma," Molly whispered in awe, like she'd seen a ghost. "I told you my Emma was coming home soon."

"Oh, Molly, stop it," Sarah said but Molly's little short legs were running across the kitchen floor and to the rocking chair where she jumped the last two feet and landed in Emma's outstretched arms.

"Emma?" Mary could scarcely believe her eyes. "When did you get here?"

Sarah shut her eyes and mouthed, "Thank you, God," before she barreled across the room on Mary's skirt tails to hug Emma. Things were going to be better now. Uncle Jed would be his old self now that Emma was home. She hadn't lied to them after all. She had simply found it necessary to stay a little longer in Georgia.

"My, oh my, what happened to my sick Molly?" Emma asked when the hugging session subsided a little bit. Sarah still sat with her arm resting on Emma's knee. Mary stood behind her with a hand on her shoulder. Molly was snuggled down like she didn't plan to leave.

"Molly ain't been sick," Mary said. "She scraped her knee on the porch when she fell down a couple of weeks ago, but it got all better when Aunt Beulah fixed some salve for it."

"Aunt Beulah?" Emma cocked her head to one side.

"Well, we called her Aunt since Cousin Beulah sounded so funny. She said it was all right to call her Aunt. She left. She just up and said she wasn't going to stay here no longer and she went back to Texas," Mary gushed. "And Uncle Jed asked her to stay a week until he could find a housekeeper but she said no and Violet came and got her."

Tuesday. Violet took her to the train station on Tuesday and she sent the telegram on her way out of town. Why? Not one bit of it made sense. No grown woman sent a horrid message like that with no reason. It's a good thing

Beulah went back to Texas because if she was standing there right then, Emma would have been tempted to shake her until her three chins blacked both her eyes. Whatever could she have been thinking of? Jed was going to be absolutely furious.

"And Anna Marie is going to have a baby," Mary kept on. "Violet says she's been real sick with something called mornin' sickness and she wouldn't want any clabber milk. She looked just awful last Sunday in church, but her husband Alford was struttin' around like he had something to do with her havin' a baby. Men sure do act funny, don't they Emma? I'm so glad you're home."

"Me, too, child. Me, too. And I'm glad nobody has been sick," she said. "But this house looks like it hasn't seen a mop in a month. We'd better get busy. What's in the smoke house for supper?"

"Smoke house is empty. We got a hind leg of deer left in the spring house. Uncle Jed said we'd have to cook it by tomorrow or give it to Buster. He's up in the field helpin' Uncle Jed and Jimmy make hay today," Sarah said. "You want me to get it?"

"Yes, I do. What about the root cellar?"

"Empty, too. We could dig some potatoes and onions are ready to bring in, but Uncle Jed has to get the hay cut and ready. We sure did miss you, Emma," Sarah said.

"Okay, girls. It's time to go to work. Mary, you fill the stove reservoir and clean off the table. Sarah, you bring in that deer leg and I'll fire up the stove. When we've got warm water, the dishes belong to you, Mary. Let's get this house cleaned all spotless, then we'll dig potatoes and onions for the roast. Is there flour and sugar around here?"

"Yes, Aunt Beulah went with Violet a couple of weeks ago and got things at the store. We've even got some of those cakes of yeast in the spring house for bread," Mary answered.

"Then bring a couple of those in with the venison." Emma shooed Sarah out of the house. "I'm going to bring in my things and change clothes. Miss Molly, you get that dust rag over there and start dusting everything you can reach."

"Okay. My Emma is home." The little girl picked up the dust rag hanging on a hook behind the stove and started on the benches beside the kitchen table. Uncle Jed was going to be so happy when he came home. She began to hum "Jesus Loves Me," only in her mind she substituted Emma for Jesus.

Jed opened the door at dusk to find a spotlessly clean house, the aroma of fresh bread and roast filling the whole kitchen, three little girls with freshly braided hair and scrubbed faces, and two blackberry cobblers cooling on the kitchen table. He blinked three times and looked again. None of it had disappeared.

Emma stepped out of the bedroom and his heart literally soared. Then he remembered how dirty he was. His hair was filled with bits of straw. He smelled horrible and his clothing looked worse than the sweaty odor of a hard-working man. "What are you doing here?" he asked gruffly and immediately wished he could bite his tongue off.

"I got a telegram two days ago. It came on Tuesday from your cousin, Beulah, saying that Molly was dying and I should come quickly." She braced herself against the wrath flowing from him.

Well, thank you Cousin Beulah. I could kiss the ground you walk on, he thought. "Molly isn't sick. Hasn't been sick. Why would Beulah do that?" Jed wondered aloud.

"Evidently to make me come back here. She's old and probably had things mixed up about our marriage, Jed. Wash up and I'll set supper on the table. We'll talk about this later. Remember little corn has big ears."

"I do not," Mary declared. "And I want to hear so I can tell it. Huh-oh." She blushed. "Can't we talk about it now? Why did Aunt Beulah tell you that, Emma?"

"This is for big people, Mary. Now, you put the plates on the table while these hard-working men wash up. Sarah, you put the silver out like I showed you. You didn't forget how to set a table while I was gone, did you?"

"No, ma'am," Sarah said, smiling brightly.

It was Mary's turn to say grace. Emma bowed her head but somewhere in the middle of Mary's long thanksgiving for everything she'd ever had and everyone she'd ever known, Emma opened her eyes to see Jed staring at her. He blushed scarlet and shut his eyes tightly but not before she saw the look in his eyes. It wasn't one of anger, like she'd thought she'd find, and that surprised her.

Chapter Fifteen

The water in the washbasin was cool. Emma remembered back at the end of spring how she'd washed with warm water. Tonight the cool water felt good on her body as she prepared for bed. A white cotton gown trimmed with ribbons and rows of pin tucks fell like a cloud when she slipped it over her head. She picked up her brush and waited for Jed. Could be he'd sleep out in the barn. Even though it was a mixed-up affair, the look she'd seen in his eyes might very well have been what she wanted to see, not what was really there.

Jed carried a pitcher of water to the tack room in the barn. He dumped it in the wash basin and stripped out of his dirty clothing. When he finished, he shaved two days' worth of stubble from his face and combed back his wet hair with his fingertips. He scrounged around in a trunk at the foot of his cot until he found clean undergarments, a plaid shirt, and a clean pair of work pants.

She heard the front door open but figured it was Jed leaving to go to the barn. That was fine with her. She might be in love with the man. Goodness knows, she almost fainted at just the sight of him standing there in his dirty clothing, but she wouldn't beg. Not Emma. She'd simply apologize for intruding into his life, tell the children the truth this time and be on her way back to Georgia. But why did Beulah do such a foolhardy thing? Emma just shook her head, picked up her hairbrush and began the last chore of the day.

"Can I come in now?" Jed whispered from the other side of the door.

Emma's chest tightened and she almost dropped the brush. She waited until she could find her voice and then said, "Of course."

Jed knew what she'd look like sitting there on the side of the bed because he'd memorized every detail the last night before she left. But the sight in reality was even more breathtaking than he remembered. Whatever made him think she was so tall to begin with? She was exactly the right height. All that golden hair flowing over one shoulder as she methodically counted the strokes. His hands itched to take the brush and finish the job for her just so he could tangle his hands in the flax-colored tresses.

"I can't imagine why Cousin Beulah did that." He slipped his suspenders down from his shoulders and unbuttoned his shirt. He hung the shirt on the back of the rocking chair beside her checked dress and thought about how right it looked there. He kicked his boots off, then unfastened his pants and laid them beside his shirt. He climbed into his side of the bed wearing only his short-all undergarment.

Emma turned around in time to see the black hair on his legs and arms, reminding her of the day they'd gone swimming and he'd played in the creek in his rolled-up work pants. "Did you tell her that I was coming back?" she asked.

"No, I told her the absolute truth, Emma. Why we married. That you just agreed to stay to help until she got here. I can't imagine whatever possessed her to do that. You must have been worried out of your mind," Jed said, stretching out in the bed until his feet hit the footboard. He inhaled deeply, the rose scent of her soap filling his nostrils.

"Well, I'll talk to the children tomorrow morning and you can take me back to the station. I'm sorry for the mess, Jed. I really am," she said.

Over my dead body, Jed thought. "Did you see a lawyer about a divorce?"

"No. Did you?" she asked right back.

He shook his head. "Haven't had time." His heart sang and his soul soared. She'd had plenty of time to start a divorce. Did that mean she was no longer interested in the rich man, Matthew?

"I've been meanin' to go to town," he said, pausing to think about how to put it so she didn't bolt like a jack rabbit and run. Just a week. Seven days to show her how he really felt.

Her heart sank to the lowest point. He was agreeing to take her back and she'd hoped against all kinds of hope that he just might ask her to stay on for a while. Give her a few weeks and she'd flush that witch, Anna Marie, out of his mind. Apparently, there was another woman by now. Well, that's just what she got for her lying vows. She didn't mean what she said, and now her chances were gone.

"What I mean is," Jed tried again. "I thought I'd either go to town or put the word out at church on Sunday that I need a housekeeper. I just kinda hated to do it 'cause then everyone would gossip about you leaving us. They all think you just went home for a little while this summer. Anyway, I guess what I'm trying to say is this. Would you think about staying a while? Maybe just 'til school starts and I can get things under control around here. Man, it's tough to get anything done with four kids underfoot."

She almost cried. Her prayer for continuance was answered. But all he wanted was a housekeeper and babysitter. He wasn't one bit interested in Emma as a woman or a wife. *You aren't my type.* His words came back to haunt her. Evidently he hadn't changed his mind in the past few weeks about just what his type could be, either.

"I'll stay until school starts," she said. "Kids look like they've grown a foot a piece this summer. I don't think I'll sew for Violet while I'm here. I'll just get them ready for school. You think you could afford to take a day next week to take us all to town? Sarah and Mary are old enough to choose fabric for their dresses. I've got money."

"I don't need your money," Jed bristled. "If the kids need clothing, I'll buy the stuff for you to make them clothing. I'll pay you."

"You don't pay your wife to do her duty," Emma told him bluntly. "Are you and Jimmy making hay again tomorrow?"

"Yes, we are. Good night, Emma." He rolled over to face the wall. Blasted woman anyway. Did he even want to be married to her? It was a whole lot easier to make her into a wonderful person when she was in Georgia. The minute she came back he realized just how sassy and vinegary she could be. *Boy, that roast was sure good for supper, and did you ever taste anything like that cobbler?* a little voice in the back recesses of his mind chided him.

"Hush," he whispered.

"I didn't say a word." Emma laid down. A hot breeze flowed through the raised window. A hoot owl sang a monologue in a nearby blackjack tree. Coyotes wailed in the distance. Buster barked at the moon. The stars were all twinkling brightly in their place. Emma was home even if Jed was a cantankerous old lizard.

"Wasn't talking to you," Jed said.

"Well, the coyotes and Buster sure can't hear you," she snapped.

"Hush. Now I'm talking to you," he said.

"Then don't tell me what to do or not to do, Jed. I'm a

grown woman and you have no right to tell me when to hush." It felt wonderful to be across the bolster from him arguing again.

"Good night, Emma." Jed's voice was as full of frustration as his body.

"Good night, Jed." Emma's voice sing-songed, full of promise.

Preacher Elgin took his place at the front of the church after the first hymn. "We are glad to see Mrs. Thomas back in services with us this morning. We trust that she found her family in Georgia in good health. We understand she went home to attend her father's wedding. We'll hope nothing else takes her out of our community again. We missed you, Mrs. Thomas."

Emma smiled brightly. At least someone missed her. Jed had been an old bear the whole day yesterday, at least the part when she saw him. That was at breakfast and supper. The girls had carried his and Jimmy's dinner up to the hay field to them. She eyed all the single women in the church while Preacher Elgin preached, using the twenty-third Psalm as his scripture that morning.

Could it be Maggie Liston after all? Was she the one Jed had set his sights on? She'd marry Jed in a minute even if he had been divorced. Anna Marie looked pretty peaked that morning but it could be that Jed was still pining for her. Whoever it was better go on home and pack a lunch, because the fight was going to be long and hard. In the end Emma was determined she would win. She'd figured something out in the last two nights when she occupied her half of the bed. Anything worth having was worth fighting for. Life didn't just happen and everyone lived happily ever after. It was up to her to make life happen and up to her to find her own happiness. Which was not a destination but a journey. Emma decided right there that she wasn't missing one step of the journey. Jed Thomas better just put his hiking boots on, because he was taking the journey with her. They'd find happiness some days. Some days they'd fight and argue. But in the end, when it was all said and done, she figured she'd look back over her life and be glad she married Jed Thomas.

"And now we'll ask Jed to deliver our benediction. We'll plan a church picnic the last Sunday before school starts. My wife says she's excited about teaching this year. You kids better enjoy these next couple of weeks," the preacher said.

Jed stood to pray. What he wanted to give thanks for was Emma. What he wanted to ask God for was wisdom in just how to go about keeping her. He said a simple prayer from the mouth rather than the heart, though, and hoped nobody else but him knew what he really wanted.

"Well, look who came dragging back to Oklahoma Territory," Anna Marie said to Emma.

"It's a strange world, isn't it Anna Marie? I hear congratulations are due and that you've been quite sick." Emma let the barb fall away from her happy heart.

"It's awful, Emma. I hate this condition. I just hope having a baby to play with makes up for it. Why did you come back? You didn't just go away for a while, did you? You were leaving for good."

"Emma, Emma." Molly barreled in between the women while Emma tried to think of an answer. "Hi, Anna Marie. Can I play with your baby when it gets here? Emma, is our baby going to come before Anna Marie's baby?"

High color filled Emma's cheeks and Anna Marie instinctively looked down at Emma's tiny waistline, cinched in with a wide belt over her deep green skirt. "Are you . . ." Anna Marie frowned.

"Huh, Emma?" Molly butted right in again. "Is our baby going to be a boy? I think I'd like a brother to play with when the other kids go to school. Then I won't be all by myself. Do you think we could get two babies at one time like Mrs. Smith got while you was gone? She got two little girls."

"Well?" Emma tried to smile but it came out more of a grimace. "You never know what might happen, Molly."

"That's right," Jed said, taking her arm and leading her away from Anna Marie. Let the girl think Emma was with child. Maybe that would keep her in her own husband's bed where she belonged. "We'd best be getting on home, Emma. Jimmy is moaning that he's starving plumb to death for fried chicken and his mouth is watering for the leftover cobbler. I swear I heard his stomach growling in church."

"Jed?" Anna Marie nodded briefly.

"Anna Marie, hear congratulations are in store. We are glad for you and Alford. A family is a precious thing." Jed slipped his arm around Emma's trim waist. "Darling, let's go home," he said.

Emma bit the side of her jaw to make sure she wasn't dreaming. Surely, Jed had simply had a slip of the tongue. He was acting like a smitten husband, and there was no way he truly felt like that. Not after the way he'd acted since he walked in the door on Friday night and found her in the house.

He kept his arm firmly around her waist until they reached the wagon, then he handed her up to her seat. "After dinner, maybe we'll take a walk around the property. I'd like to show you what all we've done since you've been gone," he said.

She bit her jaw again. Yep, it hurt like the dickens. She wasn't dreaming.

"Jimmy and I've got several more days of hay. Hope we can get it all in by the time school starts. Jimmy's worked hard all summer. I think maybe he does deserve a day in town. Maybe even a little money to jingle around in his pockets for candy at the general store," Jed kept talking.

"Maybe a pair of boots like yours, Uncle Jed." Jimmy picked up in the middle of the conversation.

"Can we go, too?" Sarah held her breath. She'd love to stroll down the wooden sidewalks beside Emma.

"Sure, we'll all go," Jed said. "And we'll eat in the restaurant while we're there. That'll be our treat for the whole summer since we haven't had enough rain so you could go swimming again."

"I'd rather swim in my swimming costume that Emma made," Mary declared.

So would I, Emma thought but she kept quiet. She might say the wrong thing and Jed would climb upon his high horse again.

Jed reached out and took her hand in his, only mildly surprised that the jolt was still there. She jerked her head around and looked at him intently but he pretended not to notice as he kept talking. "We fixed this fence. It was falling down and now we've got the whole section fenced in. See those yearlings. I think we'll butcher the biggest one when frost finally comes. And there's six hogs that'll be ready for butchering. Hot as it is right now it seems like it isn't ever going to be cold enough to stock the smoke house."

Buster romped through the wildflowers with the children chasing after butterflies and each other. Bright red Indian paintbrush, yellow black-eyed Susies, sunflowers taller than Emma, and pale pink buttercups hugging the ground made for a brilliant show. It wasn't the well-tended gardens of Crooked Oaks, and the section of ground was small compared to the thousands of acres that made up the plantation. But it was home and Emma was at peace. At least she would be if she could figure out just what was going on in Jed's mind that Sunday afternoon.

"Why are you doing this?" she finally asked. If he got riled then he could just get over it. If he was simply playing with her emotions to get her to babysit then she deserved to know. If he was truly courting her like it seemed, then glory, hallelujah.

"Because it's a glorious Sunday. Look, Emma, off to the southwest. I believe those are rain clouds. Rain in July in Oklahoma. Now that would be a miracle," he said.

"Rain anywhere in July is a miracle. And you didn't really answer my question," she said.

"I'll answer it later when the little corn with big ears is sleeping soundly," he promised with a brilliant smile, his green eyes twinkling.

"Is that a promise?" She smiled back at him. Could it possibly be that he was courting his wife? It would sure make things easier since if he didn't start courting her soon, then she'd take the initiative in her own hands and court him. After all, she was a liberated woman.

"That, sugar, is a promise," he said.

Chapter Sixteen

Supper lasted forever. The children begged to stay up late and for Emma to read them a story. The sun practically refused to set in the west, hanging there like a big orange ball of irritation. One part of Emma wanted to hear what Jed had to say; the other part dreaded it. He'd held her hand and the sensation sent her higher than the dark storm clouds still approaching from the southwest. She just hoped a tornado didn't arrive right in the middle of whatever he had to say.

Finally, the kids were in the loft and Jed went out to sit on the porch while she had the first turn at getting ready for bed. She heard him whistling softly and the noise got fainter and fainter until she couldn't hear it anymore. When she looked out the front door, she could see a pale yellow reflection in the window of the barn where his tack room was. The shadow of his form on the window made her gasp as he peeled his shirt from his muscular body. He unbuttoned his short alls and for a moment she wished the window didn't end at his waist. He poured water into the washbasin and began to clean his body.

"Whew!" She fanned herself with the back of her hand. If she was going to be finished with her own bath, she'd better get busy. She forced herself into the bedroom, where she began her nightly ritual. Off with the skirt and blouse, the camisole, her corset, and the lace-trimmed drawers. A quick cool bath with her rose soap. She'd have to gather the fall rose petals if she planned to have more of it, or else beg Eulalie to send her some from Atlanta. She'd be wanting for a lot out here in the territory, but she'd have her soap, by hook or crook. Because she'd caught Jed inhaling deeply when he stood close to her that afternoon. If rose soap was what it took to make him think of her as a wife and not a big tall horse of a woman who wasn't his type, then she'd have rose soap and take a bath in it twice a day.

On with the gown and down with the hair. She picked up her brush and had just sat down on the bed when she heard his gentle knock on the door.

"Can I come in now?" he asked.

"Of course," she answered.

Ritual as usual. He removed his shirt and laid it beside her skirt. Then his pants, after kicking his boots off. He stretched out with an audible sigh on his side of the bed and shut his eyes.

Emma waited and brushed. Brushed more and waited. He'd said he'd tell her what he had on his mind and she was wise enough not to wade into the issue and raise his ire before he had a chance to form the words. But this waiting was about to drive her insane. Finally she pulled her legs up on the bed and sat cross-legged on the other side of the bolster from him. The sheet was pulled up to his armpits and he had his hands folded over his chest. Heavy dark lashes were shut over his eyes so she couldn't begin to tell what he was thinking. Or if he was. He might very well already be asleep.

Well, if he was, he'd better get ready for a rude awakening. They might argue until morning, but when dawn came, either Emma was going to be packed and ready to leave or else she was staying forever. This was going to be her home and her heart was going to belong forevermore to Jed Thomas, or she wasn't going to stay around and watch it break into a million pieces. She'd just have to break one last vow and that was the promise to stay until school started. He'd have to understand that she couldn't remain in the same house and the same bed with him another night. Not if she was just the housekeeper and babysitter.

"Wake up, Jed." She reached across the bolster and tapped him on the chest with her silver-backed hairbrush at the same time a jagged bolt of lightning lit up the sky, followed by a clap of thunder.

"I'm not asleep," he said.

"The little corn is, though, and you promised me some answers," she reminded him.

"Ask and you shall receive," he said, intoning like Preacher Elgin.

"I'm not asking anything. You are going to talk to me and tell me what's in your mind and heart, Jed Thomas. From Friday night until this morning after church, you've gone around like you were about ready to commit murder and then you do a complete turnaround and act like I'm really your wife. So you talk to me," she said.

"Okay, I'll talk. Then you'll talk, Emma. We've got to get this settled. When I went to town that day back in the spring and we got married, I'd been praying real hard. I knew we needed a woman around here. I wanted a wife but Anna Marie was so high-tempered, and besides, I just plain didn't love her. She was available and seemed like everyone thought we should be a couple, but the sky didn't light up when I kissed her."

"You didn't love her?" Emma asked.

"No, but I was thinkin' on asking her to marry me any-way. I figured she'd do as well as anyone else," Jed said. "Then you know what happened. We were married and I kissed you and the whole world stood still. Fireworks went off in my head and I wanted the kiss to go on and on. But you didn't want to be here so I figured that kiss didn't affect you the same way. If it hadn't been for Molly, you would have left that next day. I felt like I was keeping you against your will, so I sent for Beulah."

"But you didn't want me here, Jed. I thought you were pining away for Anna Marie and couldn't wait for me to be gone so you could marry her," Emma said.

Jed's eyes snapped open. Surely he hadn't heard her right. Could she really have cared about him even before she left? "Then you left," he continued, "and Anna Marie came in the middle of the night and tried to get me to commit to her. I told her to go home and marry Alford. Lord, I'm glad I didn't marry that woman. Poor old Alford is going to have a rough row to hoe."

Emma set her jaw in a firm line. She'd have to watch that vixen Anna Marie if this baby didn't tame her down. Once Emma was a real wife, that woman better keep her claws away from Jed or she'd have a real catfight on her hands. Emma didn't start a fight she couldn't win.

Several moments of silence followed while each of them digested what the other had just said. "Then," Jed began again, "Friday there you were and I was nasty dirty, all sweaty, and you looked so cool and beautiful. I wanted to take you in my arms and kiss you again like the morning you left just to see if it felt the same, but I couldn't touch you, not in the condition I was in. The house was nice. Supper smelled scrumptious. But it was you, Emma. You'd come home without me begging so it had to mean you wanted to be here with us . . . with me. Only you'd just come because Beulah lied about Molly and it just made me mad enough to chew up fenceposts. I wanted you to be here for me, not Molly. I figured out why Beulah sent that message. Why she left. It was to bring you back here for me. She was a wise old girl after all."

"But Jed," she started.

He held up a hand to stop her. "Let me finish. Two nights I laid here beside you and prayed real hard for God to tell me how to make you love me. Me. Jed Thomas. Just a poor old dirt farmer with a section of land. Not a fancy plantation or even a banker's job. Why would you want to live here? I asked myself over and over again. It's nothing but work from dawn to dusk. Kids to raise that aren't even yours. A cantankerous man who can't see past the end of his nose most of the time, who argues with you on every issue. Not one thing to make you want to stay. Then this morning I overheard what Molly said and you didn't tell her you weren't going to have children with me or that you were going back to Georgia on the next train headin' south. I guess something just snapped inside me and I realized that maybe I did have a chance. Do I, Emma?"

He'd said all the right things except the three little words she wanted to hear so badly. He could have skipped the whole speech, simply took her hand in his and said, "I love you, Emma." He wanted a wife and a mother for the children, even children of his own. But she'd sworn she wouldn't marry or even stay married if she couldn't do it for love.

"Jed, I've been miserable. I didn't want to leave. I kept thinking you'd ask me to stay. There was a young man on the train," she paused. Another clap of thunder and it began to rain. A soft rain in spite of the bluster of a storm somewhere in the distance. Rain at the end of July in Oklahoma. Miracles did happen after all.

His heart fell. She was about to tell him that she'd found someone else after all. Not that shifty-eyed banker but a young man on the train. She had just come back to see about Molly after all. He'd hoped from the way she didn't take her hand from his that she was of the same frame of mind he was.

She cleared her throat. "Anyway, he reminded me of you and at first I thought you'd come to bring me back. But you didn't. You didn't write or anything so I gave up hope. Then the telegram arrived and I hurried back here, worrying all the time. When you weren't here and the house was in such ill shape, I was afraid you were at Molly's funeral. Then the girls came in the back door giggling. I couldn't wait for you to stop work and come home that evening. Just to get to look at you. I didn't care if you were dirty and sweaty, Jed. It was all I could do to keep from falling in your arms like a possessed woman. But Jed, you've got to understand the way I feel. Do you remember what I told you about leaving home that first time?"

"Yes, that your father was going to force you into a loveless marriage and you didn't even like Matthew." Jed nodded.

"Well, Daddy and I settled that issue. Matthew showed his true colors at Daddy and Eulalie's engagement party. I wouldn't marry Matthew because I didn't love him, Jed. And I won't stay married to you just to be your wife, either."

What was Emma saying? he wondered.

"Do you understand me, Jed?" she asked.

"No, I'm afraid I don't." He looked at her quizzically.

"I'd come to resent the work if I'm doing it just to be your wife. I won't be married to a man who doesn't love me, Jed."

Jed frowned. He'd just told her he loved her, hadn't he? He'd bared his very soul to the woman. *But you didn't say those words,* his conscience said bluntly. *A woman needs to hear those words at least once a day, twice wouldn't hurt. And you've not said them at all.*

He sat up in bed. He reached across the bolster and took her hands in his. "Emma, I'm so sorry. I love you, darling. With all my heart and soul forever. I never thought I'd find a woman I could love as much as I do you. Just touching your fingertips makes me weak in the knees. I want you to be my wife. Will you marry me? We can have a church wedding and tell everyone we're doing it again for the fun of it. I'll go to Georgia and get married on your plantation. Just don't leave me again. Without you my life is nothing."

He didn't take his eyes from hers, scarcely blinked while he waited. His future hinged on what Emma said right then.

"We are already married, for better for worse, in sickness, in health, until death parts us, I think is the words the sheriff said. But they were lying vows, Jed. Just something to keep us both out of trouble." She loved the mushy feeling in the pit of her stomach as he held her hands in his. "I don't want another wedding. I just want to be married to you. I love you, too, darling. So now I want you to hear my real vows. They aren't pie-crust vows, either, and I don't intend to break them. Not ever. From this moment, Jed Thomas, I give you my undying love. Forever and even past that. Into eternity. Through this life and the one to come. I don't promise a happy-ever-after love, but I promise to do the best I can each and every day for you, those four children, and the ones we'll produce in our marriage. And those are not lying vows. They are true and I mean every word of them."

Jed squeezed her hands and looked deeply into those strange-colored aqua eyes, lit up by flashes of lightning. "I promise to love and protect you until my dying day. I will love you forever, Emma Thomas. When we are in heaven together, we will look down upon our children and grandchildren and know we lived each day to the best of our ability. These vows aren't pie-crust promises, either. They are not meant to be broken and again, I love you with my whole heart. Now may I kiss the bride?"

"No, but you can kiss the wife," she said, leaning across the bolster. His hungry lips met hers and his soul found the mate it had been searching for.

"Can we do that again?" he asked when they broke away.

"Yes, lots of times. But first there's something I've wanted to do for a long time." She grinned impishly.

She picked up the bolster and tossed it in the corner. She slid across the bed and snuggled into Jed's open arms. Nothing would ever separate them again.